BRUT

HAROLD JAFFE

BRUT

WRITINGS ON ART & ARTISTS

GRAND RAPIDS, MICHIGAN

BRUT
Copyright © 2021 by Harold Jaffe
ISBN: 978-0-99-915355-0
Library of Congress Control Number: 2020943393

First Anti-Oedipal Paperback Edition, November 2020

www.rawdogscreaming.com

Cover Design © 2020 by Matthew Revert
www.matthewrevert.com

Layout by D. Harlan Wilson
www.dharlanwilsonn.com

Author Photo by Katana Blue

Anti-Oedipus Press
Grand Rapids, MI

www.anti-oedipuspress.com

BOOKS BY HAROLD JAFFE

NONFICTION

Revolutionary Brain

Beyond the Techno-Cave: A Guerrilla Writer's Guide to Post-Millennial Culture

Nazis, Sharks & Serial Killers

DOCUFICTION

BRUT: Writings on Art & Artists

Porn-anti-Porn

Sacred Outcast: Dispatches from India

Goosestep

Death Café

Induced Coma: 50 & 100 Word Stories

Anti-Twitter: 150 50-Word Stories

OD

Paris 60

Terror-Dot-Gov (visuals by Katana Blue)

15 Serial Killers (visuals by Joel Lipman)

False Positive

Son of Sam

NOVELS

Jesus Coyote

Othello Blues

Dos Indios

Mole's Pity

FICTION COLLECTIONS

Sex for the Millennium

Straight Razor (visuals by Norman Conquest)

Eros Anti-Eros

Madonna and Other Spectacles

Beasts

Mourning Crazy Horse

CONTENTS

ACKNOWLEDGMENTS

Gratitude to Sebastian Bennett and Shane Roeschlein for their valuable editing suggestions.

"Bob Flanagan Sentenced" first appeared in *Rated RX: Sheree Rose with and after Bob Flanagan*, edited by Yetta Howard (The Ohio State University Press 2020).

For Frantz Fanon, heart and mind

There was a man whom Sorrow named his friend,
And he, of his high comrade Sorrow dreaming,
Went walking with slow steps along the gleaming
and humming sands, where windy surges wend.

—Yeats

QUEEN OF HEARTS

The Queen of Hearts was in a cluster of a hundred women each of whom resembled her.

They were performing the Ghost Dance imagining that it would protect them from the white genociders even as the mounted US cavalry was advancing.

They were all shot dead but for one who continued to dance faster faster with madness in her feet.

Her face was a white mask war-painted with mustangs and buffalo.

She Ghost Danced and refused to die.

In my dream she was the Queen of Hearts.

BLACK ORPHEUS

1975. E and I live in the Guatemalan highlands. Maya country. I am working on my first novel in which Orpheus and Eurydice play crucial roles.

The novel is partially based on the 1959 tragic samba film, *Black Orpheus* (*Orpheu Negro*), shot in the Rio favelas during *Carnaval* and directed by Marcel Camus, no relation to Albert Camus.

One night E and I change cots because unexpectedly I'm having a violent allergic response. In each other's cots we are fine.

The following afternoon after a typical downpour I am on my old Olivetti at the window of our small casita working on the scene in which Eurydice is abducted by Death and transported to Hades.

Looking up, I see E, smiling, graceful in her long dress, moving lithely through the lush garden—*disappear*. She stepped onto a boarded-up old well, the wooden boards sodden from the rain; I watch the boards give way and my lover disappear.

I remember my precise response: *Was it "real"?*

Was it the passage I wrote suddenly come alive?

But then I was up, outside, she was about fifteen feet down balancing on outstretched hands and legs, seemingly inches from the well water, her eyes were closed and she was still, as though in shock.

And here is something odd: With her deep in the well, close to death, I feel for an instant the impulse to leave her there, let her perish.
I recover instantly.
I ran out into the road, stopped a lorry, and the Quiche workmen worked quickly, hoisting her up on a long rope.
She was bruised and silent and remained mostly silent for the few weeks until it was time to return to New York.

I thought of my strange hesitation before helping her and remembered certain versions of the Orpheus legend which assert that Orpheus deliberately turned in his ascent to earth. Left Eurydice in Hades knowing he would be cut to pieces by the maenads, but knowing that his song to Eurydice would continue eternally.

The Orphic synchronicity remained even while living in New York. Whenever we would hear a track on the radio from the intoxicating *Black Orpheus* musical score written by Antonio Carlos Jobim there would seemingly be another "occurrence," which even entered our dreams—E's and mine.
How to describe these occurrences?
Near accidents, unexpected visitors, waking visions, unprecedented dreams . . .

The exquisite young black actors, Marpessa Dawn and Breno Mello, who melded so naturally had never met until they were cast as Eurydice and Orpheu in 1959.

Nor did they see each other again until each died in 2008 on different continents, just minutes apart.

When you removed the gag that was keeping these black mouths shut what were you hoping for? That they would sing your praises? Did you think that when they raised themselves up you would read adoration in the eyes of these heads that our fathers had forced to bend to the very ground? Here are black humans standing, looking at us, and I hope that you will feel the shock of being seen. For three thousand years the white man has enjoyed the privilege of seeing without being seen.

—Jean-Paul Sartre on the film *Orpheu Negro* (1959)

PASOLINI

About Pier Paulo Pasolini, a contemporary said, "He was compelled to live dangerously in every sense, this passionate, brilliant, contradictory man."

Filmmaker, poet, novelist, Marxist, homosexual, living and trying to love in mid-century Italy.

See the shining contradictory facets in his remarkable face, all angles: pointed one way beautiful, another way pitiful, a third way saintly.

Pasolini visited the *ragazzi*, poor boys in the slums on the outskirts of Rome, paid them for allowing him to love them.

After years of these regular visits one Sunday he met friends for luncheon, seemed more or less as usual, phoned his mother with whom he lived, then drove to the outskirts of Rome.

In the next reel he is found dead, his trousers at his knees, his testicles crushed, his face and body burnt with violent wheel marks over it.

The official finding concluded that Pasolini visited his *ragazzi*, antagonized them somehow, after which they murdered him savagely, driving his car back and forth over his burnt dead body.

■■

Years later a theory floated: *Pasolini deliberately provoked his sordid murder to demonstrate the dread "meaning" of life, employing himself as shaman.*

I believe that strange story and in truth admire it. I think of other figures who might get themselves murdered to demonstrate a principle. Rimbaud comes to mind. Simone Weil. Lorca. Artaud. John Coltrane. Vincent Van Gogh, of course.

GIACOMETTI

Alberto Giacometti lived and made art in the same small, cramped Paris studio in the 14th arrondissement for forty years.

Once, crossing the street to go to the café for his twice-daily coffee, he was struck by a car, one of those armadillo-like Citroëns that only the French can drive.

It was yellow.

As Giacometti was being struck by the yellow Citroën, he thought to himself: Finally something is happening to me.

At that period he was constructing plaster images of figures no larger than his thumbnail.

Sculptures, he said then, had a likeness only when they were extraordinarily small.

Nonetheless, he added, "their dimensions revolted me."

In truth, much had happened to Giacometti since he came to Paris from Geneva by way of Stampa, Switzerland, near the Italian border, where he was born.

He collaborated with borderline psychotic Georges Bataille and was a favorite of the self-appointed chieftain of the Surrealists, Andre Breton.

Bataille and Breton despised each other and were notoriously critical of contemporary artists, though uncommonly fond of Giacometti.

Giacometti also maintained a friendship with the brilliant dour JP Sartre without serving as a Sartre acolyte.

Giacometti was commonly identified as the exemplary existentialist artist.

He did not consider himself either an existentialist or a surrealist.

His portraits of Sartre oddly resemble his portraits of the acerbic Stravinski, with whom Giacometti was also on excellent terms.

The only other gifted visual artist I can think of who won difficult people over without cultivating them or even necessarily welcoming their allegiance was Marcel Duchamp.

Giacometti and Duchamp, dissimilar as artists, resembled each other, psychically, so to speak.

Each had an extraordinary head.

The sort of head a gallery goer could view admiringly from every angle.

But their heads were no less different, one from the other, than their visual styles.

Giacometti's head projects an indisputable (if elusive) sentiment from the heart.

Duchamp's head—aquiline, marmoreal—resembles the death's head of a prince from a mythical kingdom somewhere in the northern regions where royal inhabitants occupy their time playing chess.

Giacometti

■■

Although he was sometimes identified as a Communist and for a time was a close associate of the avowed Communist poet Louis Aragon, Giacometti repeatedly said that his art was generated neither by philosophy nor ideology.

Giacometti painted and sculpted for one reason, he said: he wanted to learn to see.

(Compare Duchamp who claimed to despise the emphasis on "retinal" art.)

Diego, Giacometti's younger brother, sat for him virtually every day for seven consecutive years.

How many sculpted and painted wedge-shaped heads did Giacometti make of Diego?

Hundreds, many hundreds.

He claimed to have never gotten it right.

Somehow Diego's utterly familiar head eluded him.

To believe Giacometti, every head eluded him, which is why he would stop in the streets and stare at a stranger's face.

It being Paris, where the *fou* is pridefully integrated into the culture, nobody seemed to mind the strange man with his grizzled head stopping, staring.

Why do Giacometti's stick figures, many of which are life-size, seem to be on the verge of extinction?

Maybe the better question is what keeps Giacometti's stick figures from fading into extinction?

A provisional answer might be endurance.

■■

Giacometti was diagnosed with cancer in 1963.

He died in 1965 at the age of 64, painting and sculpting until the end.

When, a few autumns ago, I visited his old studio in the 14th, it had been turned into an apartment complex.

There wasn't even a plaque to commemorate the forty years he labored there.

"Labored" may be the wrong word; "dreamt" is better.

Of course, dreams of a certain register amount to inadvertent labor.

In Giacometti's instance, his "dreams" were an inadvertent, visionary labor, though he surely would have rejected the elevated designation "visionary."

After his diagnosis of cancer in 1963, Giacometti was reported to have said: *The terrible thing about dying is that you can do it only once.*

NO / NOT NO

Sylvia Plath was attacked because she compared her emotional pain to the Holocaust, with a capital H.

Susan Sontag observed that though the Soviets were everywhere advertised as the arch enemy of Capitalism, Capitalism adored the Nazis because they were charismatic like sharks and serial killers.

Elizabeth Costello, Coetzee's protagonist in *The Lives of Animals*, insists that the meat slaughtering industry is equivalent to the Holocaust, with a capital H.

When a writer asked Kafka how he was faring, K's response was: I consider it a blessing to simply stand in the corner and breathe.

Crazy Horse, Sioux warrior and priest, was murdered young; he didn't permit himself to be photographed. His burial place has never been revealed.

About William Blake, who distrusted the French, Bataille said "he was a man who never pursed his lips."

Simone Weil said in 1940, as countries were knuckling under to fascism, that she felt as if the center were shredding.

We are in 2020, the center has shredded.

SIMONE WEIL

Felt compelled to swallow the sputum from an impoverished tubercular patient.

She was admitted to the prestigious Ecole Normale Supérieure with the highest test scores in her class (Simone de Beauvoir scored second highest).

After graduating with honors in philosophy she became a teacher in various girls' lycées in remote areas of France.

Because of her persistent involvement in workers' demonstrations, she was transferred from lycée to lycée.

Simone Weil abandoned teaching.

She ceased communication with friends and colleagues.

Though sickly, she worked in factories to experience first-hand the deprivations of "ordinary" people.

Through the intervention of a Dominican priest she found arduous physical work on a farm in the Ardèche.

At the same time she set about learning Sanskrit, the classical language of the Hindus.

Wherever she was, she lived ascetically, fasting, sleeping on a straw pallet, reading by candlelight.

Though her family were secular upper middle-class Jews, progressive and charitable, Simone Weil was unceasingly critical of Judaism and the Old Testament.

Adversaries labeled this "Jewish self-hatred."

But that would unjustly discredit an extraordinary, if radically eccentric, humanist whose most intimate identification was with Jesus.

As a child Simone Weil would eat sparingly in honor of the hungry poor.

She went to Mass regularly and yearned to imitate Christ, but she would not convert to Roman Catholicism, she proclaimed, so long as the Vatican privileged wealth and status.

She abandoned her pacifism and traveled to Spain in 1936 to fight with the "people" against Franco.

Her family, including her mathematically gifted brother and Simone Weil herself, managed to escape Vichy France and settle in New York in 1942, but she returned to Europe only a few months later to join the "Free French" resistance headquartered in London.

Until April 1943 she wrote polemical anti-fascist reports and essays for the Free French.

In that year she entered a hospital in Kent where she was diagnosed with tuberculosis.

She refused to eat out of respect for the starving multitudes throughout war-torn Europe.

Thus she commits suicide by starvation and is buried in a small grave in Ashford Kent on August 24, 1943.

Thirty-four years old.

■■

Simone Weil wrote these prophetic words toward the end of her brief life:

Unless supernatural grace intervenes, there is no form of cruelty or depravity of which ordinary, decent people are not capable, once the corresponding psychological mechanisms have been set in motion.

ROTHKO 66

It is 1971 in the Age of Aquarius, a carefree blip in the Kali Yuga, tens of thousands of years of cruelty / misery / ass-backwardness. Last year the Abstract Expressionist Mark Rothko was found dead in a pool of blood on the floor of his Bowery studio, having hacked deep into his arms and shoulders with his palette knife.

He was 66 years old and the story was that there were 66 hack and cut marks on his body.

It was remarked that the symmetrical dark red pool of blood in which he lay, approximately six feet by eight, was eerily akin to one of his own canvases, a somber color field, though with uneven edges.

Last year he was a suicide. This year his fame is broadcast far and wide.

Rothko would make that exchange, so hungry was he for recognition.

Rothko considered himself a tragic myth-maker and longed for that exalted calling to be everywhere witnessed.

■■

But what of other artists who cut and shot and abused their bodies? The Viennese Actionists, ORLAN, Hannah Wilke, Fakir, Chris Burden, Marina Abramovic? Weren't they doing approximately what Rothko did? Yes and no. They mostly circled around death, counting on it not happening. With Rothko it was endgame.

I am 24, living on Jane Street in the West Village, two streets east of the lordly Hudson.
I am walking from my apartment to the Frank Lloyd Wright-designed Guggenheim Museum on Fifth Avenue and 89th Street to view a major retrospective of Mark Rothko's paintings.
Wright's museum opened in1959, boldly designed as a continuous ramp.
Measuring a quarter of a mile, the ramp loops around a central large atrium topped by a huge domed skylight.
In Wright's design a lift takes visitors to the top of the building and the long ramp then entices them to saunter back down.
The interior walls are curved and somewhat convex, unreceptive to hanging pictures.
Wright's idea was that his design be foregrounded; he wasn't concerned with hanging pictures.
The Guggenheim reportedly spent several million dollars to reconstruct the walls so that pictures could subsequently be hung.

I walk from the West Village to Frank Lloyd Wright's museum on 5th And 89th Street, just south of the Jewish Museum at 5th and 92nd Street, just north of the Metropolitan Museum at 5th and 82nd.

My hair is long, my black beard is full. I am tall and lithe and sockless, wearing tan clogs from Sweden.

I'm 24-years-old, I can walk miles in the handsome uncomfortable clogs.

Mark Rothko was born Marcus Rothkowitz in Czarist Russia (now Latvia) in 1903.

He escaped the pogroms by emigrating with his family in 1913 to Portland Oregon, which at that period was an epicenter of progressive activity in the US, the area where the revolutionary Industrial Workers of the World was strongest.

As an adolescent Marcus Rothkowitz along with his anarchist family attended IWW meetings where they met Emma Goldman and Big Bill Haywood.

He referred to himself as an anarchist even when he was admitted to Yale, changed his name to Mark Rothko and later became widely identified as a leader of the Abstract Expressionists, a designation he loathed.

"I'm not an abstractionist. I'm interested only in expressing basic human emotions: tragedy, ecstasy, doom."

Rothko's minimalist, intensely refined use of color without figuration associated him with the "Color Field" painters—Morris Lewis, Kenneth Noland, Barnett Newman, Helen Frankenthaler . . .

Rothko rejected that designation as well.

He used color, he insisted, instrumentally, solely as a means of conveying his subject.

At architect Philip Johnson's instigation, he and Rothko collaborated on a church designed by Johnson in Houston.

Rothko contributed 14 thematically related paintings to the church. After Rothko's suicide the church became known as the Rothko

Chapel, a privileged space of visionary esthetics and meditation, which continues to attract pilgrims from around the globe.

Despite Rothko's insistence that he was a life-long anarchist, it came out after his death that he was in the employ of the CIA.

He was not alone.

According to Frances Stonor Saunders' *The Cultural Cold War: The CIA and the World of Arts and Letters* (The New Press 2000), TS Eliot, Andre Malraux, Stephen Spender, Cszelaw Milosz, Bertrand Russell, Robert Lowell, Dizzy Gillespie, Peter Matthiessen, George Plimpton, Mary McCarthy, George Orwell, Lionel and Diana Trilling, Jackson Pollock, Mark Rothko . . . all professed progressives, with the exception of royalist anglophile Eliot, were in the employ of the CIA.

They received funding from the CIA in exchange for "combating Communism" (however implicitly) on the cultural front.

Also outed was the well-known art critic and unrelenting champion of Jackson Pollack, Clement Greenberg, who was not chagrined.

He argued that artists have no choice but to rely on patrons to support their art; whether the patrons are royal dukes, wealthy industrialists, global oil corporations, or the CIA matters little so long as strong art is produced.

I'd known that Rothko murdered himself but didn't know the details until I was scanning a volume in the Guggenheim Museum bookstore.

I don't remember the title, but it included a few pages by the novelist Bernard Malamud, a friend of Rothko, who wrote a disarmingly heartless note about Rothko's suicide.

Malamud could not comprehend it on any level, especially the extreme self-loathing suggested in Rothko's alleged 66 hacks and cuts on his body.

Melancholy Rothko was of the tribe of Hamlet; Malamud was not and lacked the sympathy to extend.

En route to the Guggenheim, I walked north on Second Avenue, then dropped into a luncheonette on 38th Street to pee.

You weren't begrudged a free pee then as you are now.

The cramped toilet was at the back of the restaurant.

I closed the rickety door and saw scrawled, almost illegible, in black crayon on the inside of the door below the doorknob:

I will kill myself today black

I peed then continued walking north.

The Rothko exhibition was imposing—the paintings lovingly mounted.

It was very crowded, viewers speaking softly with seeming intimate knowledge of the canvases.

Just last year before he killed himself Rothko had complained bitterly about the attention lesser artists were receiving while he was ignored.

After an hour or so of viewing the paintings, smelling the expensive perfume, I began walking down to Jane Street, this time on Third Avenue to have dinner with my girlfriend, Elke, a dressmaker from Sweden.

Elke was as tall as I, athletically slender, broad-shouldered.

She didn't wear perfume but her skin always smelled fresh with, curiously, a hint of nutmeg.

We ate at a bistro, I didn't mention the Rothko exhibition.

Then we went to her studio on Horatio Street, smoked dope and made love.

That night on Horatio Street I dreamt of animals, which wasn't unusual.

In this dream, though, the creatures were wild and despised and ruthlessly treated: badger, sidewinder, scorpion, shark, jackal, crocodile . . .

They—all of them—were somehow physically leaning on me, as if expecting me to intercede.

In the dream I understood what that intercession signified.

When I woke a single image was in my chest: the black crayon scrawl low on the inside door of the cramped luncheonette toilet.

I will kill myself today black

After the dream I remembered an event which happened three years before.

I'd spent a month at a compound in Nevis, West Indies, where I became friends with Harvey, the Afro-Nevisian who looked after the large, somewhat run-down property. When I was preparing to return to the US Harvey broke down and wept. A month of friendship touched him so deeply.

At that time I was studying for a doctorate in literature but was less interested in the degree than just studying.

I also wrote prose and poetry.

An early volume, unpublished, I called *Freaks' Dreams*.

I imagined and tried to inhabit the dreams of the variously dispossessed: death row inmates, humans accounted mad, acromegalic "giants," quadriplegics . . .

I recognize now that my interest in "freaks' dreams" was connected to my emotional recognition of the message to me on the
cramped toilet door:

I will kill myself today black

Other humans who used the toilet would not notice the scrawl, or
if they did, would treat it as a random graffito.

I knew—or felt—that the "plea" was addressed to me.

Not that I was to commit suicide, but that I was to intercede on
behalf of this evidently black human's potential suicide.

Intercede on behalf of the dispossessed who were prepared to
murder themselves.

An extraordinary presumption, but that's how I felt.

SUICIDE BOMBER

We turned the corner slowly and there, crouched in the headlights, was a man with a black and white headscarf masking his face.

He was laying a roadside bomb, a crude-looking device that appeared to be bound with Saran Wrap.

It was easy to imagine the man putting the thing together in his kitchen, which made it all the more menacing.

As we motored slowly through the pocked narrow streets we observed more masked men and boys in the darkness, several carrying automatic weapons.

The Hamas fighters were on patrol.

Their enemies, the Israeli army (IDF), had moved into Rafah the night before.

Tanks sat in formation at the end of the main street.

IDF soldiers were ransacking the Tel Sultan neighborhood in a hunt for "terrorists."

For the Israelis, Hamas is a constant deadly threat.

From its ranks come suicide bombers, men and boys—and, increasingly, women and girls—who have murdered hundreds of

Israelis on buses, in cafes, in malls.

People in Rafah see the Hamas fighters and suicide bombers in a different light.

To them, these men and women with their black and white checkered keffiyehs masking their faces, with explosives strapped to their chests, are heroes.

They confront Israel's tanks and jets and helicopter gunships and they die in large numbers.

In death they are honored as martyrs for the cause of Palestine.

Their faces are revealed on posters plastered on Rafah's walls.

Prayers are recited for them at the central al-Awda mosque, a dense cubic structure that resembles a fortress.

From its minaret fly the black and green banners of the fighters and martyrs.

When the bodies, or body parts, emerge from the mosque, the march to the cemetery begins. It is led by a pickup truck with loud-speakers that blare out demands for revenge.

On the south side of town the Israelis have been demolishing the small houses they say Hamas use as cover for attacks on IDF forces.

We met an old lady in a black veil trying to salvage what she could from the ruins of her bulldozed house.

Down the narrow alley her neighbors were convinced that the Israeli bulldozers would be back, that their houses would be next.

They loaded worn-out televisions and pots and rugs onto donkey carts.

As they labored, the air was filled with the sound of gunfire from nearby streets.

The old lady in the veil raised her voice above it.

"They call us terrorist," she said.

"But they are the terrorists.

"They kill our sons.

"They drive us from our homes."

When we met an adolescent boy named Asim, we asked him what he thought when he saw the armed and hooded Hamas fighters and suicide bombers move through the streets.

"We call on God to give them victory," he said.

"Would you become a suicide bomber?" we asked.

"If it is God's will, yes, I will do as they."

In the eyes of the people in Rafah, the fighters and bombers are standing their ground.

That is important because like all Palestinians they are haunted by memories of a terrible retreat.

As many as a million of them left or were expelled from their towns and villages in what is now Israel in 1948, the year the Jewish state was founded.

For some Palestinians the journey into exile ended in the tents of the Rafah refugee camp at the end of the Gaza Strip.

And the town that has grown out of the camp remains infected with an almost palpable sense of grief.

Still, families from different villages have managed to remain together for nearly three generations.

We camped in an area where the streets were descendants of what was once the Palestinian village of Barbera.

The people told us that the old place, once famous for its grapes, has become part of an Israeli township, not far from the city of Ashdod.

One afternoon we watched an old man move slowly up the alley on a donkey cart.

He was selling grapes, and he chose to make a joke on these people of long-lost Barbera.

"Grapes," he called out.

"Grapes from Barbera."

A younger man squatting under the bombed ruin of a building away from the glaring sun called back, "Barbera and its grapes have all gone."

"I know," said the old man, suddenly passionate.

"Everything is gone.

"Everything."

'TRANE

When John Coltrane visited Nagasaki in 1966, Nagasaki had not recovered emotionally from the US atom bomb attack three days after the US bombed Hiroshima in August 1945.

When the car transporting John and Alice Coltrane pulled up to the greeting area in Nagasaki, Alice got out but 'Trane stayed in the car playing notes on a flute.

The Japanese host looked into the car and asked him what he was doing.

John Coltrane whispered that he was trying to find the right music to commemorate Nagasaki.

Later, a Japanese jazz fan asked Coltrane an odd question: "What do you expect to be ten years from now?"

'Trane answered at once: "A saint."

John Coltrane died the following year, 40 years old.

YOUNG BRANDO

I got a job in the garment district on 7th Avenue pushing huge wheeled carts of furs and fabrics from factories to wholesale manufacturing outlets.

Since it was only about three miles from Jane Street where I was staying, I walked to work at 7 a.m. and walked back to the Village at 4:30 or so.

The work was hard, I didn't like messing with animal fur, and the wage was insultingly low, but I mostly enjoyed it because I got to see and work with black people and Puerto Ricans.

The person who made the strongest impression on me was a tall black man named Neville, originally from Barbados.

He never said his surname.

Neville was in his late thirties and well spoken, but because he was black, educated in Barbados and independent-minded, he could not even land a halfass job in New York.

Neville and I sometimes met after work, drank coffee and talked. Neville was an activist connected with some group or other; I never got the exact name.

Neville was against racism in any form.

He was against capitalism and how it favored class.

At the same time, he was a patient man, graceful and peaceable in his movements, with a soft voice.

He was tall and thin with long articulate hands.

I think of Neville as both a friend and a man of wisdom.

It is a little hard to summarize what he said to me. It had to do with following my instincts, trying to channel my anger into forms that were constructive, and having respect for people—especially the poor who have suffered and whose families have suffered for no justifiable reason.

He spoke of the difference between the law and justice, which I had sensed but was never able to articulate.

I've never been a patient human and Neville—mostly by the way he conducted himself—helped me to be more patient.

Neville also had a tender regard for animals.

Once when we were leaning against our carts smoking, a stray little marmalade cat emerged out of the clamorous traffic and brushed against his leg.

The big man immediately got on one knee to pet the cat.

When the cat responded to his petting, he picked it up and put it under his jacket.

I looked at him. "You're adopting the cat, Neville?"

"Yes."

Whenever I'd talk with Neville after that I'd ask after the cat, a female he called Molly.

I saw Molly again when Neville invited me to his small studio apartment on 136th Street and Lenox.

He fixed food for us, Barbados style, fish cakes, okra, tamarind, sweet coconut water to drink.

Molly drank the coconut water too.

While we were eating, some of Neville's friends dropped by— intellectual-looking black men and women, a few of the men wearing dreads.

They talked about a protest gathering they were planning at the Columbia University School of Law.

What they said was that Ivy League Columbia bought up adjoining neighborhoods in Harlem and were going to evict residents without compensation.

These residents were in every instance black and working-class.

Neville and his group, along with Harlem spokespeople, were trying to intervene peaceably.

I remember having the urge to ask if I could join them, but I held back, thinking if they needed a white 19-year-old with a hair-trigger temper they would ask me.

Three or four of Neville's comrades had some coconut water or beer with us.

Banks Beer, from Barbados.

Several of the black women associated with Neville's group were appealing, but they didn't seem interested in me.

After four months I quit the pushcart job and at my sister's urging enrolled in the New School to study with Theodor Erlacher, the exiled drama theorist from Berlin.

Because Erlacher's class was filled, I was assigned to his associate, Estelle Rosen.

It turned out to be the best thing that could have happened to me.

And it wasn't the end of my friendship with Neville, who attended a few of my performances and would meet me for dinner.

Then something came up that turned me away from acting and

everything else. Neville and his group were captured with dynamite in their possession and a blueprint of their intended target—the Columbia University Law School.

That was the official story I read in the New York Post.

I was stunned.

But I had no way of getting in touch with anyone who knew Neville Colgrave (his surname, according to the Post).

It was even difficult to find out where he was held.

Finally, I did find out and visited him in a holding tank in the South Bronx where he was being detained until the trial when—according to the news report—he and his group would be sentenced to long terms—probably life without parole—in a federal prison.

Dressed in an orange jump suit, he greeted me through the inmate's grate.

The inmates on either side of him were also black; so were their visitors.

Amazingly, Neville seemed composed and asked me questions about my acting. I turned the conversation to his situation.

"Is there anything I can do to help? Will there be bail? I can try to raise money."

Neville smiled and shook his head.

"They're going to put us away for the rest of our lives, Marlon. What you can do, what I'd like you to do, is continue the fight. It's not just Columbia buying Harlem. There are a whole lot of Columbias—bigger battlefields. And the poor are not permitted to fight back. However you can, help them to fight back."

We touched fingertips through the grate.

Two days later I read that while the other inmates in the holding tank were at chow, Neville stayed behind and hanged himself.

I wept.

I kept away from Estelle's classes and didn't answer the phone.

I went a little crazy.

I boozed like my mother and old man.

I'd hit a bar, drink myself into a stupor and pass out.

When I came to, I'd be transformed into Mr. Hyde.

I got into brutal fights in and out of bars.

I landed a construction job but was fired after I brawled with the foreman and broke his nose.

After getting fired I slept late, read a little, lifted weights at a YMCA, then drank, brawled and womanized into the dawn hours.

One night, bombed on Jameson's, I got into a brawl over a woman in a bar near the Bowery.

Before I could get set, the guy broke a whisky bottle and slashed me across the face.

Someone took me to St. Vincent's Hospital's emergency room, where they sewed me up.

Seventy-nine stitches.

I slept for two days.

When I was awake and halfway alert my sister and I talked. Instead of reading me the riot act, Lonnie mostly listened.

I tried to explain my feelings about Neville and she seemed to understand.

She said that Estelle Rosen had phoned several times about the possibility of a major part in a Broadway play.

That seemed strange—I'd forgotten that I was a so-called actor.

QUEEN OF HEARTS

The Queen of Hearts wears camo, her face is Kabuki white.

Her clothes and body are slick with gasoline.

She lights a Cuban cigar with a table match then uses the lit cigar to set herself on fire.

Ablaze, with the cigar in her teeth, she leaps from the roof of the Hotel Theresa onto the busted pavement at 125th Street, Harlem.

Nobody sees her or wants to see her.

She is beyond salvage.

Unlike Saint Joan, who cries out to Jesus, the Queen of Hearts is silent as the fire consumes her.

Her body disintegrates completely except for the faint outline of a cross.

Either a cross or a swastika.

There on the busted pavement.

NINA SIMONE

An estimated 4,000 people were rallying in inner city Newark in Fall 1964 in memorial to the three young civil rights workers: Chaney, Goodman and Schwerner, lynched in Mississippi by the KKK and the Mississippi police. Nina Simone, young but with her authority intact, was at the piano with a microphone orchestrating, energizing, governing the huge rally in speech and song.

Her unflinchingly brazen "Mississippi Goddam" was the centerpiece of her 1964 debut album for Philips, "Nina Simone in Concert," dedicated to the 1963 murder of Medgar Evers and the 1963 bombing of the 16th Street Baptist Church in Birmingham, Alabama, that killed four young black girls.

Nina Simone confessed that her first impulse on reading about the murder of the four black children in Birmingham was to take a gun to the streets and "kill someone—I don't know who—someone who was destroying my people." And when, in 1965, she was introduced to Martin Luther King on the march from Selma to

Montgomery, she reportedly said to him as they shook hands: "I am for, not against, violence in our struggle." Throughout her life Nina Simone's affinities were less with MLK than with Malcolm X, Stokely Carmichael, Angela Davis, and the Black Panthers.

Nina Simone was born Eunice Waymon in Tryon, North Carolina, to a large, poor, pious family. To disguise herself from her disapproving parents she became Nina Simone and got a low-paying gig playing piano in an Atlantic City nightclub.

How did the 20-year-old from the North Carolina backwaters end up in Atlantic City?

In Tryon, North Carolina, Eunice was a pianist prodigy at age three, playing the church organ the next year, and as an adolescent studying classical piano with a European teacher who moved to Tryon specifically to work with her.

She was six years old and presenting a piano concert at an assembly hall in Tryon; her parents were in the front row. But when more white people showed up her parents were moved to the back. Eunice saw this and immediately announced to the audience that she refused to perform until her parents were moved back to the front. They were.

With the aid of her hometown community Eunice accumulated the money to enroll in the summer program at the Juilliard School of Music in New York as preparation to applying for a scholarship at the prestigious Curtis Institute of Music in Philadelphia. By all accounts, her audition at Curtis was received favorably and her parents, evidently assuming the scholarship would be granted, moved to Philadelphia to live with her. When the Curtis Institute rejected Eunice Waymon it was a blow which Nina Simone then and for the rest of her life bitterly attributed to institutional racism.

Beginning with Bessie Smith audiences have been gifted with extraordinary jazz and blues black female singers. Still, Nina Simone's rich contralto, depths of passion, and elegant phrasings are inimitable. Why then don't we hear more of her on radio jazz stations, or even hear her name cited?

Several reasons: Her fierce commitment to racial justice enlarged her musical range while driving many conventional listeners away. She sang jazz and blues, but also folk songs like Odetta and African songs like Miriam Makeba and racial justice songs like black road-gang convicts in the Deep South.

And there was her physical appearance. Unlike, say, the creole beauty of Billie Holiday, Nina Simone's appearance was esthetically unfamiliar to most white Americans, less African-American than black African. It was a foreign or exotic look, which Nina Simone would never stop fretting about, and which she tended to accentuate with intricately braided hairpieces and colorful African gowns, all of which alienated or even frightened white American audiences.

Another contributing factor was Nina Simone's public manner which was passionately volatile. Unlike most singers she would often talk to the audience while performing, and her talk was edgily rhetorical, authoritative, unpredictable, sometimes directly addressing and even insulting someone in the audience who seemed not to be paying close attention. All of this made audiences decidedly uncomfortable, especially in the US, which is a critical reason for her increasing performances in Africa, the West Indies, her moving to Switzerland, and ultimately living and dying in southern France like her close friend and companion in arms James Baldwin.

Nina Simone was married twice, in 1958 to the white "beatnik" Don Ross, which was dissolved rapidly and about which not much is known, then in 1961 to the light-skinned black man Andy Stroud, who retired early from the police force to become Nina Simone's manager and the father of her only child, Lisa Celeste. That marriage ended in 1970.

Lisa Simone Kelly has written candidly about the agonizing love and admiration she had for her immensely gifted, troubled mother.

CLARICE

The American poet Elizabeth Bishop, living in Brazil in the 60s, wrote to her colleague Robert Lowell about an "exceptionally gifted" Brazilian writer, who, though, was very "skittish, seemingly nervous about human contact."

She was referring to Clarice Lispector, who wasn't Brazilian by birth.

Clarice was born in the Ukraine to a Jewish family that moved to Brazil to escape the pogroms when she was an infant.

In her early twenties Clarice married a Brazilian diplomat and for the next decade and a half traveled in Europe.

She returned to Brazil after her divorce in 1959 where she lived and wrote until her untimely death in 1977.

Because Lispector often wrote about the poor and dispossessed, as in *Hour of the Star, Passion According to GH*, and in her weekly newspaper column "Cronicas," there is the impression that she was "progressive," a compassionate heart-mind artist.

That is true and untrue.

■■

In *Hour of the Star*, which features the homely, impoverished Macabea, Lispector writes movingly on Macabea's behalf but also with a cruel irony "against" her; that is, on behalf of the cruel culture that ignores or destroys the vulnerable poor.

Lispector writes similarly in her "Cronicas" published weekly in a Brazilian newspaper for nearly two years.

It is as if, shaman-like, Lispector inhabits the cruel cultural position to interrogate that position from the inside-out, except the interrogation never quite develops.

In her difficult, strangely meditative fiction-nonfiction book *Passion According to GH*, the white protagonist is for unclear reasons at odds with the black Brazilian woman who works as the protagonist's maid, then abruptly leaves, having deposited a symbolic anti-colonialist mural on the wall of her small room.

The protagonist, closely resembling Lispector, remains in the room and proceeds to have a mostly hostile "dialogue" with a cockroach, the insect at least partially representing the absconded black maid.

Lispector's recent biographer, Benjamin Moser, argues that the author became involved in witchcraft.

Clarice was interested in witchcraft, which has a presence in the poor areas of Brazil, but she was far from involved in it.

There is something about the nature of her intuition, its volatility, its unpredictability, that resembles witchcraft.

Lispector is a mosaic of seemingly opposing attitudes and sensibilities, instant mood changes without psychological reflection.

That is the crux: Clarice's visionary ability is evocatively outside her control, which is how she prefers it.

That uncontrollable faculty appears to offer her some protection.

One can see it in her person, in the few interviews that have been recorded.

She has a remote beauty about her face, and her talk is disembodied, as if she is speaking out of a dream or vision.

Ordinarily, when a human possesses this quality, it has been honed by meditation or devotion of some kind.

With Clarice, it appears otherwise.

Her Cassandra-like intuitions have an ejaculatory rawness about them.

She writes in her Cronicas that "exceptional human beings are more exposed to danger than ordinary people."

Hence that "skittishness" that Elizabeth Bishop remarked in her letter to Robert Lowell.

Clarice's 1973 quasi-novel translated as *Agua Viva* is, as her avid admirer Helene Cixoux, puts it, "a narrative without a spine."

One reads it in a "circle," Cixoux says, and has to "leap" to follow, insofar as following is the point.

What follows is a clause catalogue from Clarice's narrative without a spine:

Mine is a story of instants
The oblique life is very intimate
I live sideways
My days are a single climax

Mine is a fury of impulses

I am pure

I am intrinsically bad

I write to you in disorder

We must respect our cruelty

Life is a strip of pavement over an abyss

I work while I sleep

My extraordinary gift for succumbing to fear

I must remember what never existed

I never feel compassion in the Spring

I have opened my hands and heart and am losing nothing

I demand an invented truth

I don't know what I am writing about

There is only one fury that is blessed: the fury of those who suffer privation

The greatest drawback to writing is having to use words

My preference is for harsh opposites

We no longer know how to receive grace

My concern is missing the news that comes in dream

A complete self is a non-self

My solitude holds in its grasp the grief of others

I look after the world

DICK GREGORY

Was a *polarizing figure.*

When I hear that reflex platitude I prick my ears.

Dick Gregory came up the long way, no surprise, born in Missouri, his mother a housemaid.

Set upon by racists when he was nine years old after accidentally touching a white woman's leg while shining her shoes.

He was smart in school and ran fast.

Landed a track scholarship to Southern Illinois University, where he set records in the mile and half-mile.

Drafted into the army out of college.

In basic training his white commanding officer heard Gregory joking in the barracks, confused him with a minstrel nigra and helped set him up as a stand-up comic.

Dick Gregory sure was no minstrel but it was too late for the white commanding officer. Brother Greg's engine was revved.

For the next sixty years Dick Gregory would combine sabre-sharp comedy with social activism—Mississippi; marching in Selma with MLK; Vietnam; South African apartheid; Native American rights; fasting for peace . . .

I'm never not moved when I hear Brother Greg joking, then abruptly his voice drops an octave as he fastens on to another human rights tragedy, such as a black church set on fire.

I'm reminded of Sam Lightnin Hopkins, East Texas, who when he pauses to talk to an audience between guitar riffs has the same timbre in his voice as Dick Gregory, then when he suddenly gets serious his voice drops an octave.

During the Vietnam protests Dick Gregory spent a lot of time speaking on college campuses.

He tells this story: In one of his presentations at the University of Wisconsin, Madison, a white student asked to talk with him privately.

"What's on your mind, Son."

"Mr Gregory, I am a draft-resister. I don't want to kill Vietnamese people, but my parents don't agree. They won't talk to me or even read my letters."

"Killing Vietnamese is against your principles, right, Son?

"Yes."

"So you are doing what you must do, whatever your parents think."

"Yes, but they're still my parents. It hurts me."

Dick Gregory sums it up it this way—not to the student but to the audience:

"If this young draft-resister blew up the physics lab at the university and killed a bunch of technicians his parents would rush to his side to try to protect him. But when he refuses to kill innocent brown humans in a country across the world, his parents disown him. How have American adults managed to get it exactly wrong?"

Dick Gregory evolved into what he had to become—Socratic logician, social activist, spirit guide, fasting until death's door for peace. *Brother Greg chief of grief when the call come he got to go.*

One of Dick Gregory's prime models, Mahatma Gandhi, who cleaned the privies of the lowest castes is long gone.
How is India faring behind their Muslim-hating, caste-proud, napoleonic Hindu PM, Narendra Modi, a Gujarati like Gandhi, serving his third term with a "full majority"?
Ask a bottom-caste Dalit. Ask a Muslim from Kashmir.

Brother Greg is dead and the world ain't no better, it's way worse.
Brother Greg is dead, Praise him!

GLORYHOLE

With your portable drill, drill a hole in any wall erected with hate and suspicion.
Thrust your hand through the hole and shake the hand of anyone on the other side who is willing to shake hands.
Don't display your face.

JOHN BERGER

"Despair without fear, without resignation, without a sense of defeat, makes for a stance towards the world that I have never seen before."

John Berger, nearly 90, visiting the Palestinian territories.
It is a conclusion he comes to after several weeks, meeting people, sharing tea, hearing the Palestinian people express themselves.
Berger addresses the Palestinians not by speaking for them, objectifying them as is usually the case, but from the subject position.

In a different text, in response to a question posed by a British teenager: *Are you still a Marxist?* Berger details a scene in which he is leaning against a fence observing four burros grazing in a field: "two mares and two foals, the size of large terrier dogs, with the difference that their heads are almost as large as their sides." Berger moves so that he is sitting in the field resting his head against an apple tree, and continues his gentle close observation: "Surrounded by the four of them in the sunlight, my attention fixes on their legs, all sixteen. Their slenderness, their sheerness, their containment of concentration, their surety."

Berger concludes: "They wander away, heads down, grazing, their ears missing nothing. In our 'exchanges,' in the midday company we offer one another, there is a substratum of what I can only describe as gratitude."

And, at last, his response to the British girl: "Yes, I am still amongst other things a Marxist." This is not the early Marx and Engels Marxism that spurns consciousness, but an elastic Marxism that features an affectionate close engagement with what remains of the natural world.

John Berger was an original-minded art historian who, age 28, wrote a defiant volume called *The Success and Failure of Picasso* in which young Berger dares to favor Picasso's very brief activist period highlighted by "Guernica," which was provoked by the fascist bombing of a Basque village.

As a novelist, Berger was singular.

His last novel *King* is narrated from the point of view of a vagrant dog called King who looks after homeless humans awaiting what they call The Big Pain.

Unlike, say, Orwell's *Animal Farm*, in which animals are employed as props, *King* is not meant to be a fantasy, or parable.

It is a realistic novel narrated by a dog.

There *is* a dream element that interfaces with the bleak realism, such that we can't always distinguish between the two.

Those familiar with Berger's work in several genres will not be surprised that *King* is a novel whose esthetic points outward, toward culture not away from it.

Not just toward culture, but toward those aspects of culture which have been made invisible, or from which people customarily avert their eyes.

King the dog is a wound dresser but his task is hopeless. The homeless, those who value tenderness more than money or power, will be bulldozed and left to die.

The barbarian bankers and industrialists will bulldoze the poor where they live, and that will be the end of it.

But is that actually the end?

Berger is someone who would agree with Antonio Gramsci, the brave Sardinian Marxist theorist imprisoned under Mussolini, who when asked about his belief, replied that he was a "pessimist of the intellect, but an optimist of the will."

When John Berger begins another essay with these words, "I want to say at least something about the pain existing in the world today," he is one of the very few thinkers we bow our collective heads to hear.

MELVILLE

Melville and Whitman were both born in 1819; Whitman died in 1892 and Melville in 1891. Each was born and lived in New York, though Whitman's final years were in New Jersey. Each wrote a collection of poetry about the Civil War, Melville's *Battle Pieces* and Whitman's *Drum Taps*. Each was in his way a "wound dresser," in Whitman's words.

They were similar in their feelings of the heart; Melville's homage to John Brown in "The Portent" is finally like Whitman's homage to Lincoln.

In the last stanza Melville writes of the hood draped over John Brown's head as he is to be hanged.

John Brown's "streaming beard" is untamed; the hood cannot cover it.

The untamed streaming beard is John Brown's revolutionary fervor, a righteous energy that cannot be suppressed.

Clearly Melville admired John Brown, as he admired Billy Budd's innocence and Bartleby's refusal to accede.

■■

Whitman was, against certain odds (homosexuality and premature physical frailty), an extroverted life-affirmer.

Melville's dominant "humor" was black bile; he was, like Hamlet, a melancholy introverted man.

Whitman and Melville never met.

Much better known is Melville's relationship with Hawthorne who was 15 years older.

Hawthorne's great-great grandfather John Hathorne was the only condemning judge at the Salem witch trials who never expressed his reservations, and Hawthorne seemed to assume the self-imposed burden of expiating his ancestor's puritan cruelty.

At the same time, Hawthorne possessed a strong dose of puritanism himself; he was a secretive man who preferred gazing from a distance to physical embrace.

The two writers had previously commented on each other's work— Hawthorne in a favorable review of *Typee*, and Melville in an extravagantly favorable response to *Mosses from an Old Manse*.

They met in the flesh in Massachusetts in 1850 after Melville purchased a farmhouse in Berkshire County.

Virtually from the start Melville's enthusiasm for the impending friendship was boundless. In his various letters we find lines such as: "Whence come you, Hawthorne? By what right do you drink from my flagon of life? And when I put it to my lips—lo, they are yours and not mine."

Especially: "Already I feel that this Hawthorne has dropped germinous seeds into my soul. He expands and deepens down, the more I contemplate him; and further, and further, shoots his strong New England roots into the hot soil of my Southern soul."

Hawthorne's sentiments are much less well-known, partly because of his reticence, in good part because his widow "redacted" many passages from his writings, including his letters.

Melville expressed enthusiasm for *The Scarlet Letter*, published in 1850, and waited impatiently for Hawthorne's reading of *Moby Dick* which was published the following year.

Hawthorne's response to *Moby Dick* itself exists only in Melville's response to the response, which was disappointed.

As Melville interpreted it, Hawthorne liked the more conventional narrative sections of the novel but was less enthusiastic about the rhetorical overflow, including the crucial chapter "The Whiteness of the Whale."

Despite all the benign associations with white, "there yet lurks an elusive something in the innermost idea of this hue, which strikes more of panic in the soul than that redness which affrights in blood."

Melville/Hawthorne's last meeting was in 1853, in Liverpool, where Hawthorne had been appointed American Consul by his school friend, now US president, Franklin Pierce.

After that meeting Hawthorne wrote about Melville:

"He can neither believe, nor be comfortable in his unbelief; and he is too honest and courageous not to try to do one or the other."

BEGUINE

During the second half of the 12th century across much of western Europe, women, single or widowed, young and old, abandoned their traditional roles as spouse, mother or nun, embraced poverty, denounced war, and commenced to live communally.

This marked the beginning of the Beguine movement.

(The derivation of "Beguine" is contested.)

The number of married women among the Beguines increased exponentially during the Crusades.

Aristophanes' *Lysistrata* springs to mind, except there are no out-sized erections in this sacred drama.

The Trappist monk Thomas Merton asked his friend, Ad Reinhardt (associated with the Abstract Expressionists), to paint him "something devotional."

Reinhardt presented Merton with a matte black canvas which if gazed at from certain angles displayed the tracings of a cross.

Black on black.

■■

Merton lived most of his adult life in a Trappist monastery in Gethsemane, Kentucky, yet always complained about noise.
I think of that as I wander through the ancient Beguine compound in Bruges south, now occupied by Benedictine nuns.
Everywhere is the Flemish admonition: *Stilte*. Silence.
Like the Quakers, the Beguines believed the flame in their heart was the Passion of Jesus, the sorrow of Mary.
Like the Quakers, the Beguines tended to the ill, indigent, deranged.
Harried and persecuted before and after the Reformation, the Beguines quietly persisted.
Gone now.

TUXEDO

You are in Paris.

Bastille Day.

Change into a tuxedo but first cut off the labels.

Take a warm bath while wearing your tuxedo.

Walk through the Bastille quartier in your wet tuxedo without labels shouting:

L'amour est mort. Vive la rage!

BLACK PANTHERS AND JEAN GENET

The Black Panthers are popularly depicted as revoltingly fierce but charismatic.

Hence they are condemned while being consumed.

The Panthers are lied about while the institutionalized liars profit from their lies.

The Panthers, we are informed, were black and insolent, wore black leather jackets, carried weapons, and claimed falsely to be on the side of the dispossessed.

Toward the end of his life, famous French underclass thief, homosexual, revolutionary writer Jean Genet, whom Sartre referred to as Saint Genet, expressed solidarity with the Black Panthers. Black and white progressives invited Genet to the US in 1970.

Angela Davis said afterwards: "We hadn't succeeded in raising a significant multiracial movement and thought Genet would help activate white progressives. When we advertised for his conference, the posters did not mention the Black Panthers. We just said Genet would speak and a huge crowd came to hear him because he was Jean Genet."

Genet started his talk in French with an interpreter at his side, making a moving appeal about how to fight racism, including the crucial necessity for white participation in the struggle against racism. After a quarter of an hour, members of the audience started to get restless and suddenly someone interrupted Genet asking him to speak of himself and his work. Genet responded: "No, I'm not here to talk about literature or my books. I came to defend the Black Panther Party."

At that, a few people stood and left. Then more people left. In minutes, more than half the audience had left the large assembly hall in Oakland. Most of the white audience simply didn't want to hear about the Black Panther Party.

Later in a Mayday Speech in San Francisco Genet advocated the development of a "tactfulness of the heart" when dealing with black people.
He pointed out that Blacks had silently been observing Whites for centuries and learned a great deal about them and their cultural background, whereas Whites did not even realize they were being observed.

"Since I have been here," Genet said, "I have witnessed many incidents of racism. Some have been subtle, but they happen constantly, constantly.
Others have been so overt they struck me in the throat."

■■

When Genet traveled with the Panthers to speak at different colleges some members of the Party were using homophobic slurs to insult political figures like Nixon and Kissinger.

One night, Genet showed up at the hotel where the Panthers stayed dressed in a pink negligee, with a cigar in his mouth.

Genet actually managed to generate a discussion on the similarities between the struggle against racism and the struggle against homophobia.

BOB FLANAGAN SENTENCED

While teaching in Brunei, the novelist Anthony Burgess was diagnosed with an inoperable brain tumor and given a year to live. Wanting to provide for his widow he began to write madly producing his best books, including *A Clockwork Orange*.

The diagnosis turned out to be wrong and he lived another forty years.

Bob Flanagan had cystic fibrosis and was not expected to survive his teens.

Instead he lived, with severely increasing health difficulties, until age 43.

Like Burgess, death's seeming proximity energized Flanagan to imagine venturesomely, break through limits.

Death is

In his performances Flanagan at his best transformed his torment into a principle of conquest.

The principal conquerer was his penis, which refused to die.

Flanagan and his dominatrix-partner Sheree Rose tormented his penis into outlandish theatrics.

To Sheree Rose's accompaniment, Flanagan nailed his penis and testicles to a board; ate his own excrement; displayed his naked wasted body in chains and shackles to audiences; suspended that same wasted body from pulleys.

His body was wasted; nonetheless he was virile.

His virility was the crucial actor in his project.

"These are bonafide boners and they feel good. When all else fails at least I know the plumbing is still functional."

Bob Flanagan's virility signaled the murdering back of the virulent disease that was murdering him.

Out-deathing death.

Was Flanagan aware of how his erotic masochism interfaced with his cystic fibrosis death sentence?

He was, he claims, playing sexual masochist games as early as seven-years-old with his nine-year-old male cousin and enjoying the feeling without understanding why.

Not just enjoying the feeling but finding it "sweet."

That dialectical-seeming sweetness Flanagan invoked his entire brief life whenever he and the other SM participant or participants "melded," as he put it.

His theoretical understanding of what he was up to became clear while he was with Sheree Rose from 1980 to 1996.

He responded to an interview question in *RE/Search* about his impending death:

"There are shamanistic cultures that believe in *little deaths* . . . [that] prepare you for the *big death.*

"Once I'd had enough sensation and gone far enough [in a performance], there was an immediate release afterwards, and I felt peaceful, calm and sharp—like I could do anything."

In her generous afterward to *The Pain Journal*, Sheree Rose mused about her love for Flanagan: That "brave and heroic heart."

That she could pay him such a compliment after his affectionate, but also critical, even cruel, pages about her in his journal, says something.

What does it say?

Cystic Fibrosis is

Reading Flanagan's *Pain Journal*, which records his last tormented year on earth, is not to respond to his art.

His constant complaints, peevishness, paranoiac fantasies about his friends' and family's neglect or betrayal.

None of that seems brave or heroic.

But his suffering was ceaseless and increasingly unendurable; even so he was able to joke and mock himself, mock the pain journal he was in the process of writing while dying.

If Bob Flanagan had been thirty-five or forty years old in, say, 1960, would he have been forging art out of his body's fatal illness?

Unlikely.

It seems necessary for culture to have passed through the AIDS panic, when every aspect of the pleasuring body was under institutional assault.

When a generation of young people were forbidden to engage in traditional sexual practices for fear of contamination.

One unanticipated result of that repression is that the body was turned into a site of struggle, a "canvas" on which artists inscribed their pain, angst, newfound pleasures.

Paper, wood, stone, metal, glass, sand, whitewashed walls, the soil of the earth.

Why not the flesh and blood body?

Artists in various countries were using their bodies in dramatic ways: Orlan in France; Chris Burden, Carolee Schneeman, Karen Finley, Fakir, and many others in the US; the Viennese Actionists; Hannah Wilke; Marina Abramovic; VALIE EXPORT; Shigeko Kubota and, irrepressibly, Bob Flanagan.

We are all sentenced to die, but for most of us death is a metaphor. For Flanagan, death was his dominant, it could happen at any moment, and it encouraged him to expand, stretch, dare, explore the precipitous edges of consciousness.

"I'm getting Demerol. But all that is is a kiss on the cheek. I want . . . some dick, some analgesic dick down my throat or up my ass . . . just as long as you make like you love me and take away the pain."

Fibrosis is the mother

Death is the mother of the imagining heart-mind that seizes, explores the outermost reaches, farthest perimeters.

With death looming, what is there to lose?

Bob Flanagan was sentenced to death at age two, at ten, at twenty. Just two cystic fibrosis sufferers on record had lived longer.

With his body under nonstop assault, every lived day was a gift with decidedly mixed blessings because of the extreme ongoing pain.

Flanagan's art attempts to regain possession of a body that is no longer his.

Erect an artistic prison which mocks and out-extremes the actual prison of his fatal illness.

"Shitty lungs filled with shit and I feel like shit."

That he habitually presented his art with charm and humor testifies to his art's shamanic-like power.

The condition out of which Flanagan created his art is, in extremis, our own condition.

Nor is our death sentence any longer deferred.

Global warming has suddenly brought death much closer.

The body is our agent but ultimately our prison.

Towards the end, Bob fantasized about castrating himself and presenting his testicles to Sheree.

Mad, n'est-ce-pas?

If the world you inhabit is itself mad, or maddening, or, finally, insupportable, then deviations, radical deviations, can be viewed as dialectical affirmations of your own sovereignty (Bataille), however short-lived.

Cystic Fibrosis is the mother of beauty

COUVADE

Lie on the shelf above me, experience my "labor" and have my baby.

After I "conceive" we will exchange places and I will experience your labor have your baby.

After we both conceive we will make love deliriously.

IRAQ AND IRAQ

Naïve liberal-minded Americans wonder aloud: Weren't we all originally immigrants? Why the uniform hostility to the millions of immigrants made homeless by wars not of their choosing?

The current millions are nearly all brown and black and a majority are Muslim.
The welcomed, or grudgingly welcomed, immigrants, who are our forebearers, came primarily from Europe. They weren't Muslim and they were white or off-white.

Islam in the West is largely equated with violence, terrorism, Jihad, even though it can be plausibly argued that Islamic violence was and is in large part reactive, a response to Christian and Israeli violent oppression.

Which is the greater act of terror: a 17-year-old woman strapped with munitions who blows up a bus and herself, or a squadron of US or NATO jets flying above the cloudline murdering scores of

innocent Muslims while consulting their monitors?
Not seeing, smelling, witnessing the blood, viscera, body parts of
the slaughtered brown-skinned children?

The Christian Crusades amounted to wholesale ethnocide generated by blind ideology.
The current ethnocide of the Muslim Middle East and Africa is
generated by fossil fuel greed, allied to blind ideology, and executed by advanced technology.

Here is one example among many hundreds of ideology masked
as news.
I found it on CBS online, with virtually identical versions on FOX
and ABC.

Brief "news" item:
Iraqi man living with his family in Calais, France, drops his two
children from his flat two stories high simply because his wife said
she wished she was a European woman. The children survived; the
father was imprisoned.

I located the original news story which read:
An Iraqi family uprooted by the US invasion has been forced to
live in exile in a foreign country in humiliating circumstances for
the last 16 months without knowing the language, without there
being a mosque to worship in, without the husband being able
to work at his profession as accountant. The mother and wife,
ill and anxious, remarked in haste that if she were a European
woman she wouldn't have to live in such conditions. The father
and husband, in frustration and anxiety, feeling that his faith was

unexpectedly betrayed, dropped his two children from the second story explaining that he wanted to save them from the same disgrace. Children survived; father was jailed.

The "truer" version is not to excuse the attempt to "spare" the children by killing them.
The crucial difference between the fake and true version is reading the tragic episode from the subject rather than the conveniently objectified position.

YUKIO MISHIMA

Completed the final volume of his tetralogy, *The Sea of Fertility*, while wearing his death shroud in the dawn hours of the day he was to commit seppuku.

November 25, 1970.

He made a point of leaving his complicated financial affairs in order.

He provided funds for the defense of three of the four retainers who would accompany him on his final day.

The fourth retainer, Mishima's lover Morita, was also to commit seppuku.

Suicide for Mishima was a complex application of blood and style, with a ritualized camp in the mix, as in his outlandish body-building photos.

As in certain excesses of his prose, which resemble DH Lawrence, with whom Mishima had much in common, never mind their radically different cultures.

Suicide for Mishima was pain-love allied with guilt for having lied to get out of serving in World War II and disappointing his rigid, Nazi-sympathyzing father.

It was allied with his doting mother and semi-secret homosexuality.

Recall the erotic elegance of the double suicide in Mishima's "Patriotism," both his story and his impressively lurid 1966 film based on the story, where the "disgraced" Lieutenant seizes on a pretext to lovingly disembowel himself in front of his compliant wife, who then stabs herself to death.

On the day of his suicide, Mishima was accompanied by four members of the *Tatenokai*, or Shield Society, uniformed, patriotic young men who practiced martial discipline and strenuous physical exercise in the spirit of the samurai.

Mishima founded the group, which he preferred to think of as his private army, in 1967, with the bizarrely utopian intention of restoring the Emperor to his feudal leadership of the nation.

Presumably to supply a cultural context for the restoration of Bushido, the code of the samurai.

Mishima, wearing his shroud beneath his elaborate, self-designed uniform, along with four stiff-backed, uniformed young retainers, made an unannounced visit to the commandant of the Ichigaya Camp, the Tokyo headquarters of the Eastern Command of Japan's Self-Defense Forces.

Once inside, they bound and gagged the commandant and barricaded the office.

Mishima strode onto the balcony, unfurled his Shield Society banner and read his manifesto to the cadets gathered below.

■■

His speech was intended to spur them to overthrow the government and install the Emperor as the supreme leader of the country. The response was unanticipated: irritated by his pretensions and heterodoxy, the cadets noisily jeered at him.

Mishima cut his speech off, stepped back into the commandant's office, stripped to his shroud and assumed a Bushido position on the carpet.

Then he cut his stomach fatally.

The seppuku was to culminate with his retainer-lover Morita committing kaishaku, ritually beheading Mishima.

However, after several attempts, Morita could not effect the decapitation, so another of Mishima's retainers, Hiroyasu Koga, drew his own sword and decapitated Mishima.

With Mishima finally headless, Morita cut his own stomach and was beheaded by Hiroyasu Koga.

Both bloody heads—Mishima's with his face scarred from Morita's aborted attempts—were lolling on the beige carpet for many hours while the police mounted their investigation.

What was intended as heroic after the example of Mishima's "Patriotism" devolved into melodrama and farce.

Despite Mishima's Bushido imaginings.

Suicided, age 45.

HUMAN SHIELD

Impelled by idealism insert your body between war technology
and its invested ethnocides.
Die.

SARTRE AND CAMUS

Were comrades who became adversaries.

It is not easy to parse their entanglement.

Each thin-skinned, their comradeship from the start was prickly, less about ideas than ego.

Ego and romance; we are in Paris, c'est vrai?

Sartre resembled a gargoyle on the facade of Notre Dame.

Five-feet tall, wall-eyed, exceedingly ugly.

And a bourgeois.

He possessed a handsomely modulated baritone voice which he used to effect.

France has a history of adoring charismatically ugly men.

Jean Gabin, Philippe Noiret, Gerard Depardieu, DeGaulle himself . . .

Sartre was a compulsive womanizer and proud of it.

He drank liquor and coffee throughout the day and evening while reading, writing, discoursing, usually in the Café de Flore on Blvd Saint-Germain.

Late at night he would have sex with one of his female acolytes.

He needed a good wash and never flossed his teeth but none of that mattered.

Sartre and his lifetime companion Simone de Beauvoir exchanged tales of promiscuity while occasionally hosting their own menage-a-trois, always with a female.

Camus, a Pied Noir (Frenchman born in North Africa), was eight years younger than Sartre, swarthy, from a poor, illiterate family. Disaffected bourgeois Sartre envied Camus' working-class roots and taciturn warrior disposition.

While Sartre and Beauvoir were making accommodating gestures to the occupying Nazis, Camus was deeply enmeshed in the Resistance.

Camus was sensually appealing.

He resembled Bogart in Casablanca.

Beauvoir found him appealing but Camus desisted.

Beauvoir's response, as it was with people who resisted her, was to disparage him.

Camus "couldn't stand intelligent women."

She worried that Camus with his "flash and dazzle"would eclipse Sartre in Paris's literary couture.

She conceded that Camus wrote well but he "had a simplistic mind" and was essentially a journalist.

About himself, Camus wrote: I don't seduce, I succumb.

He danced seductively in front of Sartre with a young woman who'd repulsed Sartre.

That same eve Camus made love to her.

Then there were the politics.

Though Camus like Sartre came to embrace communism, Camus subsequently renounced it in favor of Algerian nationalism.

Sartre worked earnestly to end French colonialism in Algeria.

Camus was ambivalent about the French leaving because of his deep family connection.

He loved Algeria with his heart and opted for anarchism against the Stalinist communism that Sartre endorsed.

Sartre acknowledged that Stalin was a tyrannical murderer but cleaved to the idea that communism, however administered, betokened a better world.

Camus could not tolerate the gulags and pogroms under any circumstance.

Sartre and his Parisian acolytes wrote scathingly of Camus' anarchistic volume, *The Rebel*, 1951.

As a result Camus fell into a menacing depression and didn't write for years.

Finally he wrote *The Fall*, in 1956, which was intended as a short story but became a brief autobiographical novel.

Camus was awarded the Nobel Prize for Literature in 1957.

Still he never recovered from feeling tarnished by Sartre and the Parisian left.

When Camus died in an auto accident, age 46, Sartre wrote an affectionate, even admiring, obituary.

Asked somewhat later how he felt about Camus, Sartre said Camus was his "last great friend."

FANON

When Frantz Fanon, the precociously brilliant Martiniquais psychiatrist and philosopher, met with Sartre in Paris and asked him to write the preface to his *Black Skin, White Masks*, several days of intense discussion ensued.

Sartre was immensely impressed with Fanon, who had studied with Merleau-Ponty in Lyon, but among their somewhat differing appraisals of the world in pain was the question of Negritude, a philosophy founded by Léopold Sédar Senghor, the first president of Senegal, and Fanon's Martiniquais contemporary, the poet Aime Cesaire.

Fanon maintained that the difficulties of being black were both connected to the generic dispossessed and different because of singularities in the black African oppression that should be acknowledged.

Sartre, the Marxist-existentialist, insisted that it would be in error not to subsume blackness into the suffering of the Jews, the Roma people, the chronically impoverished everywhere.

■■

One image invariably comes to mind that enforces my admiration of Frantz Fanon. With the heartening scent of revolution in the air, black African heads of state hold a pro forma meeting in Lagos in 1959 and one by one state the politically obvious.

When Fanon, unofficially representing the Berber country Algeria though neither Muslim nor Christian, prepares to speak to the other heads of state, someone in the audience remarks later that Fanon's manner immediately suggests that he won't spout blandishments.

With a severe earnestness, Fanon addresses in broad but astutely precise terms the necessity for a pan-African revolution. Then, partway through his delivery, he breaks down and sobs.

QUEEN OF HEARTS

Bussed north from Guatemala through Belize into Quintana Roo, the eastern portion of the Yucatan Peninsula.

She got off at Akumal, just north of the Maya ruins of Tulum.

Fanning south from Cancun, she avoided the tourist hotels.

She rented a room on a tiny pension in the low-lying jungle.

Gazing through the small cracked window of her room at dusk she saw nineteen toucans in single file, one after the other, flying languidly from the west to the east side of the jungle.

Someone said there were alligators in the mangroves.

The Queen of Hearts lay nude in a mangrove swamp in the jungle denseness.

The next day she bussed to Cancun.

Checked into Hotel Jesús Intercontinental, which was also a theme park.

She bathed, made herself beautiful, and that evening at 7:45, she mounted the six-story Mary Mother of God Barn, filled with theme rides and "recreations."

She launched herself into the moist salt air.

She lay sprawled, exposed and bloody on the turf below.

CHE / FIDEL / CAMILO

President Ike and the US administration were copacetic with dictator Fulgencio Batista ripping off the Cuban people, torturing political prisoners, turning Cuba into a raunchier Las Vegas, cutting the US in on the swag. But Central America and the Caribbean were full of authoritarian US lackeys, and the US wasn't all that wound up with Batista.

Moreover, the early word was that Fidel, Che, and the Cuban revolutionaries wanted to make nice with the US, even though there were contradictory signals that Fidel was moving toward the Left, as in his attempts to nationalize US companies and investments in Cuba. Not surprisingly, Vice-President Richard Nixon seemed especially suspicious of Fidel Castro's motives.

It was with decided reservations, then, that the US government invited Fidel and his delegation of bearded cigar-smoking revolutionaries to come to New York in April 1959, stay at the Waldorf Astoria, and meet some of the US movers and shakers. Che

Guevara, who was reportedly busy exporting the revolution to Africa, was not among the delegation. Nor was the third Cuban guerrillero leader Camilo Cienfuegos, who would die in a plane crash later that same year.

The Waldorf Astoria was where the dictator Batista stayed when he was wined and dined in New York, so Fidel rejected the Waldorf. Another recommended fancy hotel, the Shelburne, demanded big money up front to protect against potential damages inflicted by bearded brown cigar-smoking warriors, and Fidel wasn't going to stand for that.

Turned out that a young Cuban guerrillero, Raúl Roa Kourí, was in touch with Malcolm X and it was actually Malcolm who worked out the arrangements for the Cuban delegation to stay at Hotel Theresa on 125th Street in Harlem. Black and Puerto Rican Harlem residents were joyful to host Fidel and his warriors; there are photos of bearded, cigar smoking young fighters in their fatigues waving from the balcony to thousands of "colored" well-wishers in the streets.

Malcolm X visited with Fidel at the Hotel Theresa, and so did a host of anti-capitalist world dignitaries: Khrushchev and Andrei Gromyko, Egyptian President Nasser, Indian Prime Minister Nehru, Ghana President Kwame Nkrumah—as well as black Americans like Langston Hughes, James Baldwin, and Jackie Robinson.

Fidel Castro was to become known for his passionate marathon speeches and the speech he presented to the UN General Assembly the next day, September 26, 1960, was the longest ever delivered at the United Nations, topping four hours. To the US chagrin, Castro delivered a withering attack on American "aggression" and "imperialism," singling out US policy toward Cuba and nations in Latin America, Asia, and Africa. Fidel transitioned smoothly from his unpleasant hotel experience to the discrimination faced daily by North American blacks, to the broader evils of "imperialist financial capital" and the "colonial yoke."

Anticipating a US response, Fidel put it that "all the explaining and apologies in the world will not erase the injury to an African delegate who is turned away from a restaurant. A daily occurrence in the United States."

A number of years later I traveled to Havana to interview Alberto Korda, the nom-de-guerre of the photographer who photographed the telegenic Cubans in New York and around the world. It was Korda who snapped the famous photo of Che, the Guerrillero Heroico, in his beret with the red star in the center, Che's handsome eyes looking out into the revolutionary distance.

Though Korda's photo was taken in Cuba in 1960 it became well known only in 1967 when Che was betrayed and assassinated in Bolivia, with his wrists and ankles severed after he was killed. Fidel celebrated his comrade's life by posting an immensely blown-up version of Korda's photo in a memorial rally at the Plaza de la Revolucion in Havana.

According to Korda, it is not true that Fidel and Che were covertly at odds. Ernesto Guevara was an Argentinian devoted to the revolution of the just not only in Cuba but worldwide, and so he gratefully refused Fidel's proposal to become second in command of the Cuban revolutionary government.

In the Revolutionary Museum in Havana there is a rousing photograph of the three guerrillero leaders, each on horseback, marching victoriously into Havana. Fidel is in his customary fatigue cap, Che is wearing his beret, and Camilo is wearing a white sombrero. Korda said that the Cuban people who celebrated the revolution responded especially to Camilo Cienfuegos because he was a working-class Cuban, the son of a tailor. About Fidel it was said that in his maiden speech before thousands of Cubans a white dove landed on his right shoulder, which prophesied a long, successful reign.

The people worshipped Fidel but recognized that he was the supreme commander, hence involved with the grand questions beyond their reach. Che Guevara, they admired, though many wondered why he was such a severe and demanding commander. But they also respected that Che was especially demanding of himself, living and dying in the campo with his chronic asthma.

Korda said that Havana doctors told Che that his asthma would kill him if he didn't stop smoking cigars. They agreed on a compromise: one cigar a day. *Buen compromiso!* Except—Korda laughed— the one cigar that Che smoked daily was as large as an infant's arm.

B TRAVEN?

Who was he? Host of theories, the most convincing is that he was a revolutionary German journalist living in Munich, writing scathingly of the early Nazis. When he was accused of sedition and about to be apprehended, he fled Germany directly to Mexico.

In and around Mexico City, B Traven, known then as Ret Marut, learned Spanish rapidly and worked odd jobs as a baker, carpenter, mechanic, field-hand, bookseller, nut grower, cattle drover, informal labor organizer.

The money he got from *The Treasure of the Sierra Madre*, his deliberately bad book, made into a bad-good movie by John Huston in 1948, starring Humphrey Bogart, helped finance Traven's revolutionary organizing.

Traven traveled into arduous, untravelled indigenous areas in the mountains and jungles. Every one of his dozen or so serious novels and shorter narratives, each written in German, has to do with the victimization of the impoverished, especially Indians. We witness this clearly in his six "Jungle Novels," beginning with *La Carreta* and ending with *The General from the Jungle*.

The sequence in those novels begins with cruelty and misery, as the Mexicans who identified with the whites in charge brutally victimize los pobres.

In one instance an indigenous father and teenage son are returning to their village after five years of working on a coffee finca. Mexican police intercept them, take their money, crop their ears and throw them into a dungeon-like jail with no intention of releasing them.

The brutal victimization continues through several of the jungle novels and actually intensifies until the mostly passive victimized Indians learn how to think and feel collectively and fight back. Once they commence to fight they are merciless to their enemy.

Traven was reported to have admired Gandhi, but there is no non-violence (*ahimsa*) in Traven's righteous killing back.

When, after half a century or more in Mexico, Traven dies around 1969, at the age of 87 or so, the Mexican woman with whom he lived for most of that time, Rosa Elena Lujan, relates what she knows about her mysterious revolutionary lover. He was a quiet, intense, small-boned man who loved animals and distrusted institutions.

EMBRACE THE BUTCHER

This memorably revolting phrase has been attributed to Brecht, by which he meant that it was necessary to do what it took, including violence and in-effect complicity with the autocrat Stalin, to improve the hellish world.

His Irish-French contemporary Samuel Beckett never employed Embrace the Butcher, but had he, he would have meant: the world's corruption is irreversible. Hence embrace the butcher to underline its vileness in order to transfigure it into art.

That is what Beckett's elegantly structured *Endgame* means to do. Not to be confused, as people tend to do, with Sartre's *No Exit*. Sartre maintained that a species of sane existence was still possible, as did Brecht.

Beckett emphatically did not. Nor did Beckett savor life. He lived a long life despite himself.

■■

Beckett might have murdered himself had he married James Joyce's brilliant, schizophrenic daughter, Lucia. Beckett was acting as "secretary" to James Joyce, who encouraged him to marry Lucia, a gifted dancer with whom Beckett had briefly been lovers in their early twenties.

At that time, Lucia was disturbed but evidently not psychotic, as she was subsequently diagnosed by Carl Jung. Lucia wanted to marry Beckett, and so did James Joyce; Beckett flatly refused, believing that Joyce himself was secretly in love with Lucia whom he was employing as a muse. Joyce did not deny it.

BANG YOUR HEAD

Access global "news" on your smartphone in the kitchen, bang your head once against the wall.

Access global news on your smartphone in the living room, bang your head twice against the wall.

Access global news on your smartphone in the bedroom, bang your head three times against the wall.

Access global news on your smartphone while sitting on the toilet, bang your head four times against the wall.

Get dressed, spray on cologne, go to work.

DADA

Imagine Dada, birthed during the massive senseless murdering of World War I, as an in-your-face senselessness.

A special kind of nothing.

Nothing as anti-meaning, as excrement, as the vomit of endless public speechifying.

There are other nothings.

The vibrating space between two Beethoven chords in his Grosse Fuge.

The asymmetrical vibrant emptiness of the raked gravel passages in the Ryoan-ji rock garden in Kyoto.

A wise human said that when being begins nothing matters.

That no-thing erupts silently into the energized matter of Buddhist meditation.

Nihilism is a brutal payback to the prevailing nothing.

Not unrelated is the nothing of suicide, void in the shape of a razor or noose or 12-gauge aimed at a chest.

A selfie.

Harold Jaffe

■■

Which points to the current ubiquitous nothing culled from Descartes and what passes for lawfulness.

Purportedly it officially commenced with "attempts to solve the *Entscheidungsproblem.*"

It is soulless and will not bleed.

If *you* bleed this Cartesian nothing will avert its gaze.

Dada was aimed at the brain and chest but was not confluent with suicide, especially before being coopted by surrealist power-broker Andre Breton.

Engaging characters infected Dada: Hugo Ball, Hans Arp, Kurt Schwitters, Francis Picabia, Meret Oppenheim, and later, the inimitable duo of Duchamp and Man Ray.

I have a special fondness for the Romanian Jewish Dadaist Tristan Tzara, small and supple and antic with his monocle and comical posing.

In one of those group photos so common among early artists in every genre, Tzara always posed in a way that set him apart—raised on someone's shoulders, with his foot in the air waving his monocle, standing on his head.

I often think of artistic brilliance in pairs: Graham Greene and Max Frisch; Roman Polanski and Charles Manson; Clarice Lispector and Emily Dickinson; Andrei Tarkovsky and Robert Bresson; Theodore Kaczynski and Jerzy Kosinski; Goya and Van Gogh; Lewis Carroll and Balthus; Brando and Belmondo; Nina Simone and Jeanne Moreau; Kathy Acker and Anais Nin; Egon

Dada

Schiele and Otto Dix.
Tristan Tzara is melded in my imagination with Jean-Luc Godard;
they never met.

MAN RAY

The genesis of Man Ray's inspirational flatiron with brass tacks glued in a column down the center includes these options:

Man Ray had another "sculpture" prepared for an impending exhibition in a Paris gallery which was stolen, so, without forethought, he bought what he needed in a hardware store and assembled "Le Cadeau" in 45 minutes in the store itself.

Man Ray had just met and befriended the charming Eric Satie and decided on the moment to present Satie with a gift. Seemingly without forethought Man Ray went into the nearest hardware store in Montmartre and purchased a flatiron, brass tacks and a tube of glue which he assembled in half an hour on the spot. Satie received "Le Cadeau" with grace and an admiring chuckle.

JAMES BALDWIN

Wrote about African-Americans having two "languages": The enforced artificial language with whites in formal situations and the crucial language with like-minds, which meant in nearly every instance like-color.

The like-minds language was creative, musical, intense. It also resembled, to Baldwin, inmates sending tap-tap codes to one another in adjoining cells.

Once the Man decoded the code, the inmates would change it to regain their privileged space.

In a, so to speak, non-prison environment, African-Americans, especially young African-Americans, speak several "languages": The rhythmic way he or she walks, the way they dance, the way the young man wears his cap.

The baseball cap was worn back-to-front, but once whitey caught on and started wearing his cap back-to-front, the black young man wore his sideways. And when whitey started doing that, the young black man resumed wearing it front-to-back.

Same sequence with acrobatic breakdancing, and perhaps strangest of all: Rap. That rap became as flexible a musical format as it did was a surprise; but that rap is now copied (mostly ineptly) throughout the globe is the biggest surprise, and again a testament to the resourceful ingenuity of the African American musician-social activists who created it from an amalgam of inspirations such as Caribbean calypso and urban trash talk . . .

I see elements of that secret "language" even in the acrobatic dunks in basketball. I'm among hoops viewers who prefer to see athletic hi-style, like dunks and ball-handling, rather than manic win-at-all-costs.

When a young black athlete is censured for paying too much attention to "hot dogging" and not enough attention to winning, my first response is: Style is Beauty; win at all costs is Capital.

Fundamentally, I see this multi-pronged African-American "language" as a socialized resistance to and defiance of the long suffering that commenced with the slave trade.

LOLITA

A retail store chain in Britain has withdrawn the sale of beds named Lolita, designed for little girls, after furious parents insisted the name was synonymous with sexually active pre-teens.

Lolita is a 1955 novel by the Russian Nabokov in which the middle-aged narrator seduces his 12-year-old stepdaughter.

Staff who administer the website selling the beds never heard of the classic novel or either of the two films based on the novel, hence saw nothing wrong with advertising the **Lolita Midsleeper Combi—a whitewashed wooden bed with pull-out potty designed for girls aged five and six.**

Until a vigilant mum who saw an abridged version of the Kubrick movie on the telly raised holy hell on a parenting website.
Were Nabokov alive, he would have paused briefly from butterfly snatching to laugh, then yawn.
He was a lifelong insomniac.

STEAK

First frame: Middle-aged white male naked from the waist up lies on his back.

He is overweight, has a smartphone attached to his belt, and wears strong cologne.

In the middle of his naked hairless chest is a porterhouse steak.

He falls asleep and snores loudly.

Second frame: Slender teens in hip-hop outfits enter his space stealthily.

They remove the porterhouse steak from his chest and substitute a large graphic photograph of a stock animal being brutally slaughtered.

Third frame: The teens are tossing porterhouse steaks from an overhead ramp onto the busy freeway.

TED HUGHES

Wind, slanting rain, north London, 9 p.m., Ted Hughes or a version of him is walking rapidly in his thug cap and mackintosh when he sees 50 yards or so in front another male walking toward him holding something in his arms.

Dog? Child?

As they draw close to each other they stop.

The man is holding a small fox in his arms.

The men look at each other in the slanting rain.

Ted Hughes and the small fox look at each other.

Hughes smells vaguely the appealing stink of the fox.

The man says to Hughes:

Do you want her? Just 5 quid.

Hughes looks at the man then at the small fox.

Were he to purchase the fox it would be off to the wild where he, or his shadow, wishes to be.

Instead he shakes his head no, hurries down to the tube, back to Sylvia, 18 Rugby Street, Bloomsbury.

■■

Except she is not there, she is lurching through the frozen streets to the public phone, calling again and again, not getting an answer.

4 p.m., Highgate, north London, wind, rain, Ted Hughes or a version of him in his mackintosh and thug cap is hurrying past a construction site, and in the filthy weather does not hear the repeated recorded warning: **Mind the gap, Mind the gap . . .**
Usually sure-footed, Hughes slips and plummets deep and hard back to Sylvia, 18 Rugby Street, Bloomsbury.

Except she is not there, she is lurching through the frozen streets to the public phone, calling again and again, not getting an answer.

DOSTOYEVSKY

Dostoyevsky, age 28, bound, blindfolded, facing the firing squad, about to be executed—then reprieved at the last minute.

For a short time, Dostoyevsky had been associated with the Petrashevsky Circle, a social-minded intellectual group critical of the Russian Orthodox church.
It was this association that led to his arrest and planned summary execution.

But what was he imagining when he was bound then blindfolded? With seconds remaining, the rifles locked and loaded, a messenger arrives on a black horse waving a white flag shouting to the shooting squad to stop the execution on orders from the Tsar.
No show of mercy! It had been planned—every detail from the blindfolds to the firing squad, to the extraordinary last-minute reprieve.
An official way of imposing torture.
Dostoevsky died 32 years after that incident but its ramifications

appeared unfailingly in his work—*Crime and Punishment*, *The Devils*, especially *The Idiot*.

Dostoyevsky's wildly energized power derived in good part from what he was imagining when he was bound then blindfolded, about to be executed.

That brilliant obsessive Thomas Bernhard wrote in his uniquely cranky memoir (*Gathering Evidence*) that once he managed to read through Dostoyevsky's *The Demons* (formerly *The Possessed*), his world changed.

Dostoyevsky's novel was for Thomas Bernhard, "wild genius."

Wild and obsessive as Bernhard's own writing rapidly evolved into.

Artistic wildness has variable characteristics, but always displays exceptional energy bordering on recklessness, obsessiveness, and a contrariness (which may or may not function dialectically).

That same artistic wildness often borders on psychopathy, what many professionals (not themselves artists) wrongly call madness.

BLAKE AND GRETA

Blake's "Holy Thursday" from his *Songs of Innocence* has the "beadles" with "wands as white as snow" guiding the children "two & two" into St. Paul's Cathedral on Ascension Day (Holy Thursday). But when the children commence to sing it is like "a mighty wind they raise to heaven." They have soared well beyond the counsel of their cautiously wise elders to merge with life at its most elevated, which is to say, life at its most fundamental.

Hence the so-called autistic Swedish schoolgirl Greta Thunberg, who, at age 15, skipped school every Friday to sit in front of the Swedish parliament with various hand-printed signs about climate change, such as:

We Will Not Let Our Parents Shit On Our Future

Her protests, even without the prosthetic Internet, have managed to spread widely, globally. Hundreds of thousands of schoolchildren around the globe are urgently, angrily, participating in their own local school strikes for climate change awareness and action.

There is in these protests a different kind of joy—the joy of struggle, of community and cooperation, instead of the ubiquitously fetishized competitive joy of "winning," which is inevitably harnessed to money, greed, materialist mania.

It is a mixed pleasure watching children leapfrog past their years of relative innocence and easy enjoyment to the grave responsibility of leading with an irrepressible intensity the largest battle we have in this rapidly failing world.

TIME

Is winding down fast.

Rush outside without your smartphone.

Stop every boy- or girl-child you see and whisper in their ears twice, clearly:

WILLIAM BLAKE! WILLIAM BLAKE!

Permit yourself to be straight-jacketed, carted away.

BUDA / BUDDHA

We were staying in Buda; the exhibition of wooden Buddhist artifacts was in Pest on the opposite side of the Danube. My companion wasn't interested so I went alone, getting lost as usual but finally finding my way.

The wooden artifacts were mostly small: Buddhas, bodhisattvas, in meditation, displaying mudras. They were old originals from East Asia, and expensive. I bought a catalogue of the exhibition, written in Hungarian. I still have the catalogue and have gazed at the photographs many times.

What I remember vividly about the exhibition was the middle-aged female clerk. We acknowledged each other silently and exchanged deep good feelings.

I have had that experience with middle-aged or older women many times in different venues. In Amsterdam, it was the disabled Sikh restaurant owner who exchanged kind feelings silently.

Buda / Buddha

When I came into the same restaurant four years later she recognized me and showed me a photo in celebration of her daughter's birthday taken four years earlier. I was in the photo wearing a blue wool sweater.

In San Francisco it was one of the Filipina women who cleaned the hotel rooms. Few words, deep kinship feelings.

Trekking In Nepal during my Fulbright year in India, the guide led us past a forest temple in the Himalaya foothills. Prayer had just broken and the head nun, or *bhikkhunī*, walked directly to me and, speaking softly in broken English, asked whether I wanted to join the temple.

I am not certain what joining the temple signified exactly, but it was the expression on the nun's face that has remained with me. Affection but especially kinship.

What if had joined her temple, remained in Nepal and India and Sikkim, become a compassionate monk? Who then would I tend to? Would I have access to the most needy? But I was a 29-year-old American, interested in the spirit but not up to the rigors, the abstinence, the anticipated great loneliness. Instead I harbored the illusion that my art-making would function like a species of Tantric Buddhism. Fiercely energized compassion.

Whitman remarked about his *Leaves of Grass* that he anticipated the book being read like the Bible. The disheartened human opens a page anywhere, reads a handful of lines, becomes encouraged thereby.

■■

At age 50, middle of the journey, Thomas Merton, writer-monk, leaves the Trappist monastery in Kentucky on a self-appointed ecumenical mission. A journey to the East with the intention of integrating Christianity, Buddhism, Hinduism, and Islam. About halfway through his journey, in Thailand, he has a bath, then touches a faulty fan, is electrocuted, dies.

Banal terminus for such a high-minded mission.

Was the electrocution an epiphany or a warning? But didn't Merton, after many years of rigorous devotion, earn the right to meet with other God-loving humans with an eye to integration?

What does "right" have to do with it?

Merton was a passionate but rigorous man who broke with Dorothy Day and the Berrigan Brothers over their civil disobedience against the Vietnam war. Merton denounced the war but maintained that active protest was not the priest's decision to make.

The Berrigan Brothers intensified their non-violent action against the war, and both were indicted and served time in federal detention. While in exile in Paris, Dan Berrigan met and collaborated with another exile: the Vietnamese Buddhist monk Thich Nhat Hanh. Their volume, *The Raft is Not the Shore*, discusses the activist spirit.

One crucial section concerns a 13-year-old Vietnamese Buddhist nun who immolated herself in protest of the war. Father Berrigan and Thich Nhat Hanh considered whether a 13-year-old was, so to speak, morally in position to murder herself in protest of a war that of course took no notice of her. They agreed that her act was immensely brave and even saintly.

A repeated dream I had during those years has me, or a version of me, sitting cross-legged in the front row of a group of monks. The lead monk is sitting cross-legged facing the monks. That is, I am "first" among the devotional monks, second only to the lead monk addressing us.

What could that mean? Moving up in the next life? And what was I doing sitting cross-legged to the lead monk's right when left was my best direction?

The decisive blows are always struck left-handed.

ROBBE-GRILLET

Taxiing from Rennes in Brittany north to St. Malo, annihilated
by US bombing in 1944 because of the occupation of fewer than
97 Nazis (US "Intelligence" claimed a battalion of Nazis), faithfully rebuilt, imposing granite ramparts fronting the sea.
The feeling woman next to me, the driver quiet, cordial.
On either side of the narrow road, Lombardy poplar, white oak,
birch, chestnut, hollyhock, hibiscus, early blossoming privet.
I roll the window partially down to smell the sweet green, instantly
recalling the mixed smells of frangipani, dung, urine, incense in
southern India half a lifetime ago.

The low-caste driver transporting me each a.m. to Sri Sharma,
my yoga-pranayama teacher in Kerala, southern tip. That
first morning in the tiny ashram, supine, in the corpse position with my eyes closed I feel a coolness on my right temple
even as Sri Sharma whispers the words *You will feel a freshness*,
touching me with a knobbed stick, shillelagh-like, that his own
master used on him. For that entire year, practicing daily when

I wasn't traveling, I never again experience freshness on my temple. My mind anticipates it, cannot sleep, will not dream. Correction: dream is what I do, shared dream the primary reason Sri Sharma and I hit it off at once. Devotee of Lord Rama and Hanuman, Lord Rama's monkey godling, Sri Sharma is himself monkey-like, supple, vigorous, a mischief-maker often at my expense, always good-natured, except when I say a few critical words about another war between India and Pakistan that erupts while I am there. When we travel together north in sacred Rishikesh the first creature I see, even before the everywhere crows, is a rhesus monkey. "Hanuman," I point and we laugh. Being driven to the airport for Hyderabad, central India, to deliver a lecture on Walt Whitman, nervous as I always am driving to an airport in any city, the taxi passes Sri Sharma's tiny ashram, I gaze and there he is standing on his head, Sarvangasana, yoga calm. I laugh dolefully.

Now half a lifetime later driving north from Rennes to St. Malo, faithfully rebuilt, the woman by my side, the quiet, cordial Breton driver, fragrant green on either side of the narrow road.
Beyond, tree and brush, farmland, extending to the horizon, distinctive farmhouses of slate and red granite, Breton style.
Gazing through the closed window, viewing the natural world through feeling's memory, knowing / not knowing where I'm headed.
Recalling the Zen monk saying with an ironic smile to us Americans in a Manhattan "ashram," trying to sit straightbacked on the floor: You Americans talk about understanding, but what you are doing is overstanding. Understanding comes from the hara not from the head.

■■

Taxiing from Rennes to St. Malo I think of the cold, cruel, gifted Breton, Robbe-Grillet, born in Brest on the western tip of the peninsula among rock, wild sea, salt fragrance of saxigrage and baby's tears, cold-blooded, combative, openly sadistic, his family anti-semitic Petain supporters, himself a trained agronomist who wrote of the pleasure of inflicting pain on others, young girls, his specialty, and on himself.

We have that in common, inflicting pain on ourselves, for different reasons, his Sadean, mine out of Kafka, Benjamin, Mahler, shamanic or sacrificial. Hence I'm joking with my friend on the crenellated roof of a tower in ancient, amiable Dinan, on the River Rance.

Driven to Dinan by Antoine, short, muscular, with tattoos and a red beard, who served in the Foreign Legion for two tours, 12 years. Djibouti (close to where Rimbaud post-poetry dealt arms), Tahiti, Martinique, Guadeloupe.

Despite his rugged look, Antoine is gentle, quiet, wanting to practice his English (we want to practice our French), apologizing for playing classical music (Berlioz) in his taxi.

I am on the crenellated roof of the tower-like monument looking far down, no one below, not injuring anyone when I slip off the edge, laudable suicide, except I am with my friend and don't want to leave her with the burden of gathering the smashed bits, flying alone back to benighted America.

She snaps me in my mocking suicide pose with her smartphone. It was Rilke, knowledgable of interior space, who wrote that death was simply nothing (no thing), the difficulty being the transition from life, such as it is.

In Brittany, then, another scribble on the palimpsest that constitutes a sort of life, as Graham Greene put it about himself.

Was there a novelist anywhere who wrote out of so many far-flung venues? Haiti, Mexico, Vietnam, Sierra Leone, the Congo, the French Riviera, the Middle East, Central and Eastern Europe, China, Cuba, Panama . . .

Greene was of the tribe of Hamlet.

He confessed (with a curious pridefulness) to regularly playing Russian Roulette as a young man.

He smoked opium situationally.

He wrote the novel and screenplay of *The Third Man* and I've wondered why he and Orson Welles who was featured in the film didn't ever communicate on or off the set.

They wouldn't have liked each other.

Greene had caste, went to Oxford, converted to Roman Catholicism but didn't stick with it.

Orwell remarked acidly that Greene could have written the same novels only better had he remained in England and fought for his country against fascism.

Nor could Orwell be pleased with Greene's quasi-conversion to Roman Catholicism, though it was a familiar gambit for British gentlemen of Greene's caste. One Oxonian becomes Catholic, another becomes Communist.

Greene's protagonist Scobie says to himself: "Point me out the happy man and I will point you out either extreme egotism, evil—or else an absolute ignorance."

Evidently it was difficult for Graham Greene not to play at grieving, as he did at Russian Roulette.

Even in his "playing" grief was not absent.

BLACK ELK

Black Elk, the Oglala Sioux shaman, was cousin to the warrior-dreamer Crazy Horse.

Black Elk recognized his shamanic calling early but was reluctant to leave the fallen world behind to become a Heyoka, the sacred clown whose prime work was to inhabit the fallen world not as an occupant but an empath or, in Mahayana Buddhism, a Bodhisattva.

Moreover, he was not certain that he was capable.

Though reluctant, Black Elk accepted his calling and accomplished great good.

LAST TANGO IN PARIS

Paul and Jeanne—Marlon Brando and Maria Schneider—meet in-advertently at an apartment for rent in the Passy quartier of Paris. Orchestrated by Paul, the two have an ongoing affair in the vacant apartment.

Paul insists they not confide anything of their past.

Paul is a 45-year-old American whose wife Rose just committed suicide with his shaving razor.

Jeanne is a 20-year-old Parisian actress.

An ineffective subplot features Jeanne and her fiancée (Truffaut's goofy alter-ego Jean-Pierre Léaud), a film director.

Dotted through the film are couples dancing the tango in an ex-travagant way to loud campy music.

You wept several times in *Tango*. Were those real tears?

Paul wept.

The tears were real.

You're one of the very few macho male stars who cry a lot.
On and off the set.
Any reason you can pinpoint?

You don't like to see Brando cry?

It's evocative.
But it makes me uneasy.
How about the fucking in *Tango*?
Was that real?

Bertolucci wanted frontal nudity, real fucking.
I told him I didn't see the film that way, so he backed off.

You wrote in your autobiography that you could not get an erection.
That your penis was reduced to the size of a peanut.

Acorn.

Sorry, acorn.

I've had problems but erectile dysfunction was never one of them.
In *Tango* my body was telling me the frontal nudity was bullshit, unnecessary.

What did Bertolucci mean when he shouted out to you on the set: "You are the embodiment of my prick?"

He didn't know what he meant until he said it.
After saying it he still didn't know what he meant.

Was your co-star Maria Schneider relieved or disappointed that you two didn't actually fuck?

Why would she want to fuck a fat old man onscreen?

You weren't that old in '71.
You weren't that fat.
You're Marlon Brando.

And you are . . .

Jaffe, the angry writer.

Angry about what?

Whaddayagot?

Would you have liked to fuck Maria Schneider onscreen?

Yeah.
Hold the butter, though.
The butter scene couldn't have been in the script.

Did you like it?

Enormously.

Simulated.

No anal penetration.

Just a little of that French sweet butter.

Though Maria said later that she'd felt violated, even raped.

What did Bertolucci think?

About what?

The butter.

Never mentioned it.

The agreement was I could improvise any way I chose.

If it didn't work we'd edit it out.

But only with my permission.

How did you get along with Bertolucci?

Technically, he's a good director.

We were on different wavelengths.

How so?

He was directing one film and I was acting in a different film.

I don't know that I can describe either one.

He couldn't either.

Though he pretended to, throwing around words like "existential" and "angst."

Justifying the Francis Bacon tableaus he used as the credits rolled.

I like Bacon's work but it has nothing at all to do with the film.

Bacon's work has nothing to do with the film you can't describe?

Nothing.

After *Tango* Bertolucci said about you that you are an angel as a man and a devil as an actor.
What did he mean?

Nothing.
Like existential and angst, it sounds provocative.

If existential and angst don't apply, why is the leading character Paul in such a rage?
Why does he weep?
Why does he insist that he and Jeanne—the Schneider character—not grant any personal info?
That they exist—however briefly—as though in suspension?

Because he values dream-space, alienation, suspension, more than so-called realtime.
Is that a foreign concept to you?

No.
Only his dream-space is fucking, which is somewhat limited, no?

You don't like to fuck?

Initially, Bertolucci wanted to cast Jean-Louis Trintignant in the leading role.

I wish he had.

Why?

I used myself up in that film.
The way I do it everything is evoked from my past, which meant recalling things I should have kept buried.
I exposed myself in a way I'd never expose myself again.
Unlike theater—serious theater—it's easy to do movies from the outside-in.
That's how I did it after *Tango*.

Were you angry at Bertolucci for encouraging you to act in that painful "method" way?

No.
It was my choice.

What did you think of *New Yorker* critic Pauline Kael's rave review of the film, especially of your performance?
She compared its impact to Stravinski's *Rite of Spring*.

Pauline Kael went off the deep end on *Tango*.
It was not even remotely a great film and I've done better acting.

Where?

What?

In which of your films have you acted better than in *Tango*?

I'd have to think about it.

Your performance in *Tango* got excellent reviews—not just from Pauline Kael.
But Bertolucci was faulted for casting Maria Schneider, who was only 20, with almost no acting experience.
Do you think the film would have worked better with a more experienced actress like Dominique Sanda or Stephane Audran?
Each was approached before Schneider, though neither could do it because of prior commitments.

Maria was fine.
She turned against the film and the butter thing years later after declaring herself a feminist and bisexual.
We got along on the set.
We're still friendly, though we don't talk about *Tango*.

What is it with Bertolucci and the tango?

It's an affectation.
Like Hitchcock appearing in an unexpected context in each of his films.
Except that's funny.
The tango shit is boring.
Bertolucci wants to be charismatic like Hitchcock or Pasolini or Godard.
He's cultivated but he's not charismatic

There are actually two anal scenes in the film—the well-known butter sequence where you sodomize her; but then a second

scene, where you ask her to trim two fingernails on her right hand then stick her fingers in your ass.
That had to have been improvised.

Yup.

Why did Paul specify that she stick the fingers of her right rather than left hand in his ass?

That's a question?

Yes.

I don't know why.

Why did you want her to sodomize you?

Not me, Paul.

What if Colonel Kurtz of *Apocalypse Now* was in Paris instead of Paul?
Would he use butter to sodomize young Jeanne?

Kurtz liked boys.
Without butter.
Kurtz wanted boys to fuck his ass.
You never read *Heart of Darkness*?

There's nothing in Conrad about Kurtz wanting boys to fuck his ass.

Coppola turned Kurtz in Vietnam into Jim Jones in Jonestown.

So?
Jonestown is Main Street.

Coppola resembles Bertolucci.

No.
They're two chubby Italians is all.

Paul ordering Jeanne to finger his ass follows a sorrowful scene with Paul's suicided wife's mother, in which Paul experiences both contempt for the world he inhabits and self-contempt.
Does he induce Jeanne into sodomizing him because of his self-contempt?

Can't say.

What about those evocative lines when Jeanne comes into the vacant apartment after a week or more of fucking Paul anonymously.
She calls out to him but he doesn't respond.
Then she sees him lying on his side casually eating bread and cheese. She says: *Why didn't you answer me?*
What makes you think that an American eating bread and cheese on the floor is interesting?
Then she says: *Your solitude weighs on me.*
It is not a generous or indulgent solitude.
You are an egoist.

You liked those lines?

Yes.

Thank Bertolucci.

You, Brando, are known for your silences—your solitude while in the presence of people.
Have you ever considered its effect on other people?

Bertolucci was right.
Paul—and Brando—are egoists.

You spoke some pretty decent French in the film.
How did you learn the language?

I've traveled in France.
Polynesians speak French.
I live for part of the year in Polynesia.

So we have an overweight, middle-aged, French-speaking American egoist fucking and sodomizing a beautiful 20-year-old French girl in a vacant apartment not just once but over a period of weeks.
Is that plausible?

Is it?

Well, it's the early Seventies.
The counterculture is still pulsing.

Everyone fucking everyone.

Paul in the film is smart and mordantly funny.

But is it the kind of humor that would attract 20-year-old petite bourgeois Jeanne?

Is it?

I think that if it's the famous-infamous Brando she's fucking, it's plausible.

If it is just Paul the American, depressed and overweight in his Camel hair topcoat and cashmere turtleneck, it's a stretch.

You could be right.

Jeanne jokes with Paul; she says in broken English: *I am Little Red Riding Hood and you are the big, bad wolf.*

Then she strokes Paul's arms and says: *What strong arms you have.*

Paul's response is: *Better to squeeze a fart out of you.*

She strokes his hairy stomach and says: *What a lot of fur you have.*

Paul responds: *Better to give a snuggling space for the crabs and lice.*

She touches Paul's mouth and says: *What a long tongue you have.*

Paul's response is: *Better to stick in your rear, my dear.*

Raunchy sort of sex, right?

And improvised.

Was Maria Schneider down with that kind of raunch?

It was just talk.

I didn't squeeze a fart out of her—as far as I know.

I didn't lick her ass.

Maria is beautiful but I wasn't feeling sexy on the set.

I'm not sure why.

Preoccupation with one of my divorces?

My children?

Maybe I just wanted to be in Polynesia.

The dead rat scene was funny, though Jeanne didn't think it was. After they find the dead rat near the bed where they've been fucking, Paul picks it up by the tail and starts joking about eating it with mayonnaise. He says to Jeanne: *I'll save the asshole for you.*

I always liked that line.

Because Jeanne's come in from the rain and is soaking, Paul says with what for a moment seems like compassion: *Better get out of those clothes. You'll get pneumonia.*
You know what happens then, right?
You die.
That means I'll have to fuck the dead rat.
That line leads to a more philosophical line where Paul says:
You have to go into the asshole of fear.
Improvised line, obviously.
What does he mean by that?

What did you say your name was?

Jaffe.

Well, Jaffe, if you're interested in Brando then you're interested in so-called method acting.
Learn something about the asshole of fear.

Unrepressing your deepest fears for the purposes of acting authentically.
But I thought that is precisely what you decided not to do after *Tango*?

The line was in *Tango*.
Even before *Tango*, but consistently after, I acted superficially and only to make enough money to live the way I want.
Or think I want.

Being considered a great actor no longer matters to you?

Never did.
Gielgud is a great actor.
Olivier is a great actor.
Barrymore—when he wasn't soused—was a great actor.
I am not a great actor and I don't give a shit.

There is the scene in *Tango* where Paul is shaving presumably with the same straight razor that his wife Rose used to kill herself.
Jeanne is in the bathroom with him and maybe a little bit freaked.
Especially when Paul makes a reference to being psychotic.

Mad.

Right. There is a sense of madness or autism in Paul's character. Was that intentional?

Yes.

You feel some affinity with madness?

Me or Paul?

Both. Either.

Yes.

**When at the climax Maria shoots Paul, he sticks the gum he's chewing on a railing before collapsing.
Another method move, right?**

No, the gum just lost its savor.

**Final question:
Were you wearing your trademark earplugs during the shooting of the film?**

Only when other actors spoke their lines.

BRUT

Bataille insists that in an insupportable world the single righteous response is to commit a "sovereign" act, such as Vincent van Gogh did when he severed his ear.

Vincent's act was not Buddhist, nor was it an imitation of Christ's agony, nor was it a tormented plea to a prostitute.

Vincent's act was a sovereign response to an insupportable world.

Antonin Artaud's pamphlet *Van Gogh: Suicided by Society*, emphatically agrees.

Mad Artaud was, with everything else, a savior.

But couldn't that apply to every artist accounted mad?

"Art Brut" was coined by the painter Jean Dubuffet in the 1940s.

Art utterly ungoverned by social mores.

Art that plummets without hindrance and soars without hindrance.

The plummet is agony but without it there is no soaring.

To plummet is the brut artist's condition.

Is the brut artist's art-making restorative or does it intensify the torment?

Here is Aloise Corbaz, Swiss French.

Born in 1886, to a middle-class family, Aloise studied to be an opera singer. As a teenager she had a passionate love affair with a young Frenchman which was cruelly aborted by her older sister. Soon after Aloise left for Germany to be a governess in an aristocratic household where she became hopelessly infatuated with Kaiser Wilhelm.

When she returned to Switzerland and started manifesting psychotic symptoms it was recommended that she be briefly institutionalized. She readily agreed and she ended up living the last fifty years or so institutionalized, dying in 1964.

It was written about Aloise that she "entered into madness as one enters into religion and adjusted herself to asylum life as a nun does to the convent." Clearly she felt and needed the space that genteel madness has sometimes afforded, especially as an artist of considerable originality. *Having nothing more to lose the brut artist can indulge in the intoxication of self-surrender and untrammeled freedom which is so favorable to imaginative creation* (Michel Thevoz).

Put another way: *The psychic operations of madness afford entry into primary processes located in the part of the unconscious normally inaccessible because of acculturation* (Breton).

The wound, the dreadful hollowness of the paralyzed self.*

Black Elk, the Oglala Sioux shaman, resisted his prophetic dreams, as did Cassandra, whose fate was to be prophetic but discredited. An unwanted martyrdom which moreover is unacknowledged, though not absolutely.

Artaud's prophecy embedded in the embattled self destroyed his body, his early beauty transformed utterly.

His torment not just embraced—exhibited.

Unwinding the bloody bandage which is the letter to his wound.

Did Artaud savor his torment?

Moments of a sour savor while buried alive.

Enhanced by the magical pipe.

Christ lives in Art Brut and so does the heart of the heart of Mahayana Buddhism.

How do you know whether your wound is prophetic?

When the cyborgian foreman shouts "Duck, sucker!" and you don't duck, your wound is prophetic.

No longer to be in control of one's anger.

John Brown, Nate Turner, Malcolm X, Crazy Horse, Simone Weil, the frail, brilliant French Jew who was more wrathful than Luther at the Vatican.

Enthralled with Jesus un-Vaticanized.

Uncontrollable anger is just even if deflected to a surrogate.

Show me a surrogate who is innocent.

Rebellion of the hanged = revolution of the just.

"You are courteous, even modest, in real time," she says. "In your writings you are a psychopath."

Mindwork among the collapse of language.

Language fatally fetishized and not just by the French.

Language is to the felt mind what law is to justice.

Bellowing of elephants, weeping of dolphins.

Grief-song the calf sings to her mother murdered for ivory.

Not the notes / the vibrant space between.

Not the Ryoanji rock garden / the unexpected spaces between.

Those disarming pauses in Beethoven's late quartets.

Death zone surrounds the intoxication

All problems are incomprehensible.

War, death, evil dreams, the erotic, transient joy, pestilence, global warming . . .

In an early film Artaud played a persecuted Jew.

Scapegoating, hate-mongering, extermination.

Provide the algorithm.

Sit with your head in your hands be silent.

Artaud was asked to present a radio speech to cultivated France.

For four hours, the story goes, he stood before the microphone not uttering a word.

Cultivated France listened without blinking.

There exists a mute password with which certain creatures pass through the gate.

Encounter with syphilis.

Body without organs.

Alma Mahler accused Gustav Mahler of "withdrawing his libido."

Mahler had the birds poisoned outside his dacha so that he could compose songs from nature.

Mahler's ardent biographer Bruno Walter denied that assertion.

Mahler's *Das Lied von der Erde*, conducted by Bruno Walter, with "real" birds deleted, is unsurpassed.

Gentle Schubert died of syphilis, age 31.

From Artaud's radio play, *To Have Done with the Judgment of God*: "When you have made him a body without organs / then you will teach him to dance wrong side out."

To free oneself from a utilitarian psychology.

Put your body between the oppressor's tank round laced with depleted uranium and the impoverished child who throws stones.

Human shield / No language.

Official psychology will ape the culture.

Neuro.

You say the globe is perishing / it is in the brain.

With courage I descend into that cave with no means of measuring time.

Now begins the game of recognizing someone I know in every face.

I am poor in mind. The points of mind I am capable of attaining are infinitely restricted.

You are the lunatic Artaud, admitted in France because it is France.

On your own terms you are "infinitely" restricted.

You fear to feel and your mind is bloodied with feeling.

Your tendency—contracted from Descartes—is to label heart *mind,* as you do with Vincent, Rimbaud, even the Marx Brothers in your appreciative commentary on *Animal Crackers.*

It was in a northwest African version of a French assembly hall when Frantz Fanon, a Martiniquais psychiatrist in his early thirties, took the podium to deliver a proclamation on behalf of pan-Africa. A listener, dulled from the platitudes of previous speakers—interchangeable African ministers and heads of state—was unexpectedly struck by Fanon's serious demeanor, his precise analysis, his sudden break in composure, nearly weeping at one juncture in his delivery.

Who was this speaker? How did his chest get in the way of opportunism?

Frantz Fanon had the courage to weep even there.

Heart-gesture to those who refuse to avert their eyes.
Wretched of the earth.

Fear is poetry.
Poetry will purge fear—temporarily.
John Berger writes of the besieged Palestinians' despair without fear.
Is that fearless despair poetry?
Is John Brown's virtuous wrath poetry?
Is a virulent, fearless wrath, such as Nazi Propaganda Minister Goebbels inhabited, poetry?
Fundamental feeling approaches poetry the closer it approaches dream.
Is dream fear?
Canonical artists admire the "brut" artist who, unmoored, can soar or plummet, no social-induced boundaries.
Is the brut artist's fear in the composing or afterwards?
Hashish provokes amusement / opium courtesy.
Another characteristic of art brut is uncanniness.
Yet another characteristic is the peculiar medium; in fact, whatever is at hand: tissues, toilet paper, wrapping paper, the institutional walls, bread crumbs.

Madness is not a phenomenon of nature.
It is an entity that varies in its definition and extent with history and civilization.
The same psychic states which, in India or New Guinea, are valued for their magic power, are declared to be diseased in our society and penalized by exclusion or confinement (Foucault).
Certainly psychosis is often generated by an agonizing breakdown,

which, at the same time, liberates an immense creative potential. The psychotic's vision of the world, similar to our own, suddenly founders and is replaced by archaic schemas. Their visions expose the peril and vulnerability inherent in every human psyche. This explains why we relate to, and are impressed by them; not because so-called psychotics are strange and incongruous but because in an obscure way they reveal things about ourselves (R.D. Laing).

God has placed me in despair as in a constellation of dead ends whose radiance culminates in me.

Call me contagion.

Shit to the spirit.

Who in the heart at the bottom of dreams.

The human face is an empty power.

My sword has nine hooks and 14 knots.

Sit with your head in your hands be silent.

To live is an infinite series of hungers.

Even the "great" moments are costumes beneath which are exchanged complicit glances.

■■

* I am responding to selected Artaud declarations (in bold) from his notebooks.

BRUT

HAROLD JAFFE is the author of nearly thirty
volumes of fiction, nonfiction, and docufiction. In
addition to *BRUT*, his anti-oedipal works include
Sacred Outcast, *Death Café*, and *Induced Coma*.
His books have been translated in France, Spain,
Italy, Germany, Japan, Cuba, Turkey, Romania,
and elsewhere. Jaffe is editor-in-chief of *Fiction
International*.

OTHER ANTI-OEDIPAL TITLES

"Only the idea can inject the venom." —Deleuze & Guattari, *Anti-Oedipus*

9 780999 153550